For fif … been acknow … ng science fiction … gazine form i … peared in hardba …
Over fi … ubs exist o … *RHODAN* fan conventions are held annually. The first *PERRY RHODAN* film, SOS FROM OUTER SPACE, has now been released in Europe. The series has sold over 200 million copies in Europe alone.

THERE IS NOW A BRITISH PERRY RHODAN CLUB. Send SAE to Dave Taylor, 15 Alwyn Gardens, Upton by Chester, Cheshire, who will send full details by return.

Also available in the
PERRY RHODAN series:

ENTERPRISE STARDUST
THE RADIANT DOME
GALACTIC ALARM
INVASIONS FROM SPACE
THE VEGA SECTOR
THE SECRET OF THE TIME VAULT
THE FORTRESS OF THE SIX MOONS
THE GALACTIC RIDDLE
QUEST THROUGH SPACE AND TIME
THE GHOSTS OF GOL
THE PLANET OF THE DYING SUN
THE REBELS OF TUGLAN
THE IMMORTAL UNKNOWN
VENUS IN DANGER
ESCAPE TO VENUS
SECRET BARRIER X
THE VENUS TRAP
MENACE OF THE MUTANT MASTER
MUTANTS VS MUTANTS
THE THRALL OF HYPNO
THE COSMIC DECOY
THE FLEET OF THE SPRINGERS
PERIL ON ICE PLANET
INFINITY FLIGHT
SNOWMAN IN FLAMES

Kurt Brand

Perry Rhodan 26: Cosmic Traitor

Futura Publications Limited
An Orbit Book

An Orbit Book

First published in Great Britain by
Futura Publications Limited in 1977

DEDICATION

This English edition dedicated to
FRANK M. ROVINSON
Author of "Cosmic Saboteur"
More POWER to you!

Series and characters created and directed
by Karl-Herbert Scheer and Walter Ernsting,
translated by Wendayne Ackerman and edited by
Forrest J. Ackerman.

ISBN 0 8600 7960 0

Printed in Great Britain by
C. Nicholls & Company Ltd
The Philips Park Press, Manchester

Futura Publications Limited,
110 Warner Road, Camberwell,
London S.E.5.

Chapter One

STRANGER FROM SPACE

'Unbelievable!' Reginald Bell finally said after Perry Rhodan's long silence finally became too oppressive for him. 'I still can't believe it!'

Rhodan only smiled bitterly, saying not a word.

Bell flared up. Here in privacy with the Chief of the New Power he could afford to talk to him as a friend to friend. They had been together ever since their first trip to the Moon in the *Stardust I* and remained friends now as the Terranian leader endeavored to pacify the Galaxy for the protection of Earth.

Perry & Reg presently found themselves, together with a few members of the Mutant Corps, aboard the heavy space cruiser *Terra. Terra* and companion cruiser *Solar System* had just emerged from hyperspace in the familiar section of the universe near Pluto's orbit. Separated by 25,000 miles, the two ships raced across the solar system toward Terra.

The shock of transition, the unpleasant side effects of a leap through space, had subsided; Perry had left the Commander of the ship, McClears, to the operation of the craft and had retired to his cabin, requesting his friend Bell with a glance to accompany him.

'Perry,' Reg erupted, '*It* has played a cruel joke on you! But why didn't you try to reach Wanderer anyway?'

Perry thoughtfully regarded Reg. 'The Immortal admittedly likes to play jokes but they are never mean, Reg.'

But Bell was wound up and wouldn't let Rhodan finish. 'Perry,' he said gravely, 'we didn't exactly go to Wanderer for pleasure but because the Springers pose such a serious threat to us. If the Springers decide to make a concerted attack on us with all their firepower it will mean the end of us. *It* has wilfully refused us admittance to Wanderer. And you don't call that unfunny, Perry?'

Perry Rhodan was extremely disappointed and dismayed, a condition in which his men never saw him. He had not yet been able to devise a method of stemming the peril of the Galactic traders. He looked past Bell, who watched him expectantly. Bell knew full well that his friend only tried to disguise his disenchantment and helplessness.

'Good heavens, Perry,' Bell muttered, 'I don't know you the way you're acting now!'

Rhodan ignored his remark as he replied, '*It* trusts in our ability more than we do ourselves – it can be the only explanation, Reggie. Remember how tough *It* made it for us on our way to *Its* planet? You and I still have to learn something about *Its* sense of humor. *It* didn't let us enter and refused to acknowledge our presence because *It* had no intention of handing over more tele-transmitters to us. It seems to be *Its* opinion that we should defend ourselves against the Springers with the means currently at our disposal . . .'

'If that's humor I can no longer appreciate a joke!' Bell replied disgustedly. 'The *Stardust* has only two tele-transmitters – that's the grand total. What do you think will happen to the *Stardust* if their friends the Mounders assault us with their overwhelming force? The *Stardust* will be no more, not to mention the cruisers *Terra* and *Solar System*, and the Earth will be an enslaved colony of the traders.'

Bell saw a gleam in his friend's eyes and a grim smile on his lips as Rhodan stretched himself vigorously, beginning to feel a little better.

'You're absolutely right,' Rhodan replied. 'If the Springers deploy the Mounders in a determined effort, all will be lost. Now if this isn't a terrific joke! *It* trusts us to beat off the Galactic traders and the Mounders to boot!'

Disheartened again, Bell sank back in his chair. 'Is that all you've got to say, Perry?' he moaned, completely deflated.

'Yes, Reggie, for the moment anyway. Thanks for being such a good friend and giving me a poke in the ribs at the right time!'

'Who . . . me? When did I do that?' He looked so flabbergasted that Rhodan told him with a broad grin: 'You don't look so smart!'

'I'd give a fortune for a hint on how to grapple with the calamities ahead,' Bell snarled angrily and then fell silent.

Terrania, the capital of the New Power in the Gobi

Desert and seat of the Terrestrial World Government, awaited the arrival of the two cruisers *Solar System* and *Terra*. After the structure disturbances due to the transition through hyperspace, the ships had contacted Terrania via hypercom and now received instructions how to traverse the force-field above Terrania.

Perry Rhodan left the *Terra* in a taciturn mood. He maintained a formal appearance by reciprocating greetings and exchanging a few words with some of the officials but he did not fool his friend Bell.

Not in the entire existence of the Earth had it been in such jeopardy as now that it had been discovered by the Galactic traders one time members of the now slowly-decaying Arkonide Imperium. They lived almost exclusively in clans on their huge spaceships and carried on trade with all planets which seemed profitable. Neither friend nor foe of any race they always remained neutral and sold their wares to both sides in a conflict for their own advantage. Nevertheless the Springers, as they were called, were no harmless roving band of Star-Gypsies. Any outsider trying to enter their domain was mercilessly exterminated. If their own considerable power was inadequate, they could call on the help of the Mounders, descendants of the Arkonides like themselves but people of incredible weight and – what was much more dangerous – possessors of tremendous space battleships.

Perry Rhodan had so far held the Traders and Mounders in check but had been unable to make the lesson *Hands off Terra or pay with your lives!* stick.

He briefed his staff of officers about the acute danger

threatening from the fleets of the Springers and the Mounders.

'The heavy cruiser *Centurio* will be christened tomorrow and put in service,' Commander Nyssen of the *Solar System* remarked hopefully.

Rhodan smiled woefully. 'What difference will it make? None! One medium size spaceship more or less – and with the *Centurio* we still have only three in this class – doesn't count for much against the massed forces of our enemies. Anyone with an idea will have my eternal gratitude.'

He looked at his aides: Reginald Bell, the cruiser Commanders McClears and Nyssen, Maj. Deringhouse, the mutants and finally at Khrest and Thora. His eyes fastened longest on the proud Arkonide woman. In the 10 years they had known each other their relationship had become ever closer but not close enough to let anybody dream that these two exceptional beings could be more than friends.

The *Centurio* was christened by the Arkonide Thora. Behind her stood Deringhouse without a muscle moving in his face but unable to hide the joy in his eyes at becoming the commander of such a fabulous cruiser.

Not far away Perry Rhodan, chief of the New Power, Reginald Bell and the Arkonide Khrest stood together in a group. As Thora loudly proclaimed the christening words, Khrest whispered to Rhodan: 'Who would have thought 10 years ago when we first met after my crash on the Moon that you'd have to defend the Earth as Administrator of the Terestrial World Government against invaders from the universe?'

Their eyes met. One individual, an Arkonide with the knowledge of an age-old civilization and the other Perry Rhodan, an outstanding, member of the human race on Earth, intelligent, courageous and heir to the Arkonide knowledge, the only man besides Reginald Bell who would be spared the process of aging in the next six decades.

As Perry was about to answer Khrest, Bell nudged him and pointed to the telecom screen. The picture grid flickered and the face of Col. Freyt appeared.

'What's the matter?' Rhodan asked quickly in a low voice. He didn't want the ceremony of launching the heavy cruiser *Centurio* to be interrupted.

Freyt noticed Rhodan's concern and restrained his loud voice. 'Chief, the structure sensors on Mars and one of Saturn's moons have just picked up something!'

Rhodan perked up immediately. *The traders!* he thought. *They took three months to prepare their attack and now they're coming.*

But Freyt interrupted him excitedly: 'Another signal, Chief! Second structure disturbance. The same ship has left the solar system again.'

'Col. Freyt!' he responded, 'give . . .'

'Call stage one alert!' Rhodan ordered quickly, glancing doubtfully at the heavy new cruiser which had just been christened by Thora.

Col. Freyt's face fluttered away from the picture and the screen turned gray. Bell chewed on his lower lip and

Khrest looked like a man holding his breath.

Now stage one alert had been invoked. However Terrania was not unprepared. The super-battleship *Stardust II* – the non plus ultra of Arkonide art of engineering which had been conquered by Perry Rhodan and his mutants on the world of the Ferrons – stood ready to join the heavy cruisers *Terra* and *Solar System* and a number of destroyer groups while others were on guard patrol between the planets.

The stage one alert remained in force while Rhodan summoned his closest aides for a consultation.

Evaluation of the report had confirmed that an alien ship had transitioned from hyperspace into the Solar system and disappeared again in another leap back into hyperspace.

Reginald Bell was beaming optimistically: 'A negotiator from the Springers, Perry . . . ?'

John Marshall, tall and dark-haired, didn't change the expression on his earnest, slim face. Nobody would have suspected him to be a telepath. He shook his head when Rhodan looked at him questioningly and said: 'I know the Springers too well to expect them to send an intermediary in the strange ship which vanished again. The Springers are concocting a plan to eliminate us in one stroke.'

'Perhaps a faulty transition . . . ?' Bell expressed his thoughts and was startled when the Arkonide Khrest remarked sharply: 'The Galactic traders originate from our race, Bell . . .'

'Too bad,' Bell retorted gruffly but then he caught himself. 'It's indeed regrettable. Otherwise we'd have much less trouble than we do with your offspring!'

Khrest resitated a moment, then he understood what Bell had meant by his words. But the remark stuck in Thora's craw. With fire in her eyes she pounced on Bell: 'You should be the last one to denigrate us Arkonides! Your attitude smacks of . . .'

She stopped in the middle of her sentence when she noticed that Perry Rhodan had trouble concealing a chuckle. Now she realized she had once again been carried away by Bell's stinging humor.

'We'll have to wait and see,' Rhodan declared at the end of the consultation. 'Our destroyers in the solar system will remain on alert. It's all we can do at the moment.'

Commander Derringhouse was liable to be found almost anywhere on *his* ship. He wandered as in a dream through the spherical craft which measured more than 600 feet in diameter.

His *Centurio* was scheduled to start on its maiden flight in an hour, at which time the mighty ship would lift off to roam through awe-inspiring space fraught with dangers.

He supervised the final checkup himself.

Weapon Control! There seemed to be only one expression in the language everybody spoke: 'All clear!'

Rangefinder system, transmitters, communication with engine room, with coverters – all clear, clear, clear . . .

When the final all-clear came through Deringhouse took a deep breath. His mind was no longer on the high alert status which still prevailed.

Perry Rhodan was a little surprised when he saw Khrest and Thora enter the room. John Marshall wanted to leave as with his telepathic powers perfected by hypno-training he recognised that the Arkonides wished to talk alone to Perry Rhodan. He had already turned to walk out when Rhodan held him back. 'Stay with us, Marshal!' he said softly, nodding to the Arkonides in a friendly gesture.

There was a quick frown on Thora's forehead. She still remained the same sensitive Arkonide as ever, resenting it if something went contrary to her expectations. The extremely tall, slim Khrest, the outstanding scientist in the Arkonide Imperium, exuded a serenity in harmony with his knowledge.

Thora's mein relaxed under Perry's steady benevolent gaze. She disregarded Marshall's presence and began to speak: 'Time is getting short, Perry Rhodan, and it is working for the Galactic traders and against the Earth – against all of us including Arkon! The *Centurio* is now ready for its first flight. Let Khrest and me fly to Arkon in the *Centurio*. I don't make this plea in order to force the fulfilment of your promise under the pressure of grave circumstances but out of genuine concern for Terra and fear for ourselves . . .'

Perry Rhodan's face had become very serious. He studied Thora and Khrest very carefully, Rhodan had utmost faith in the scientist but because of her impulsiveness he did not trust Thora enough to exclude ulterior motives.

John Marshall stood closely behind the Arkonides. With a supreme effort of his telepathic abilities he had succeeded in gaining access to the shielded brains of the Aliens and deciphered their thoughts. When he glanced at Rhodan the sign was understood.

'I know,' Rhodan replied, reassured by Marshall's information, 'that I still have to make good my promise ...'

'But this isn't what matters now,' Thora interrupted vehemently. 'We want to get help for you, Perry Rhodan. Help which *It* on the invisible planet Wanderer has denied you. But my people, the Arkonides, will not fail us. Only by rallying the might of our race will you be able to withstand the onslaught of the Springers and the Mounders!'

'Their attack can occur any minute.' Rhodan tried to avoid a decision although he had told himself many times already that now the time had come when he was in desperate need of outside help.

'Perry Rhodan!' Khrest confronted him. They looked at each other. 'Rhodan, I'm disappointed in you. You're evasive. You can't escape fate by subterfuge. Thora and I must go to Arkon at once! The *Centurio* is ready to take off. Let us go or don't you trust us any more?'

It was a harsh question for Perry Rhodan. After all he owed all his knowledge and power to these two people.

Then he impressed the Arkonides with his frank reply: 'It's true I wanted to delay your flight to Arkon but not because I mistrust you. I was still hopeful of finding a way to repulse the Springers without assistance from others. Now I realize that this will be impossible.'

Marshall broke in: 'Chief, a message!'

'Yes,' Rhodan responded, turning his head to the telecom where Col. Freyt's face wriggled onto the screen.

'Chief!' Freyt said agitatedly. 'The transceiver station on the Moon has intercepted a call coming from the same sector where the two structure disturbances were observed to have taken place yesterday.'

'The message, please!' Rhodan demanded.

Quickly Freyt conveyed the call: 'Levtan requests the Lord of the New Power Perry Rhodan to give his permission for landing. Please reply on same frequency. Levtan.'

'Thank you, Col. Freyt!' Rhodan called back, his face beaming. Freyt failed to understand why his boss was so happy with the message.

'I guess we won't fly to Arkon after all?' Khrest inquired apprehensively before Perry could say a word to the Arkonides.

'Not yet, Khrest!' In the same breath he turned to John Marshall and said: 'You heard the communication. Inform Bell and tell him to take care of the evaluation!' Then again to the Arkonides: 'Just a minute, please!'

Perry Rhodan had been famous since he was a young cadet in the U.S. Space Force for his ability to make instantaneous mental switches. This talent had been further improved. He alerted all stations in a few seconds with terse commands via telecom. His instructions reached far beyond Pluto's orbit, where the destroyers were on guard patrol.

Chapter Two

'TREACHEROUS ANGEL OF PEACE'

Reginald Bell, Perry Rhodan's friend and deputy, let his stocky figure fall onto a chair, pushed a stack of radio message evaluations aside and grinned at Kitai Ishibashi, the Japanese physician and psychologist.

'We've got work for you, Ishibashi. We're expecting company soon. Somebody wants to see the Chief. He's inquired...'

'A Springer?' Kitai Ishibashi asked. His almond-shaped eyes lit up briefly.

'Perhaps a Springer. Probably. We don't know yet. But when his ship arrives we'll depend on you and you'll have to stay on call. Our future hangs in the balance and your skill may make the difference.'

'I'll do my best,' Kitai Ishibashi assured him.

Bell looked thoughtfully at him. He was very apprehensive at the thought that a Springer's visit was imminent. There was something highly peculiar about it but neither he nor Perry Rhodan could put his finger on it.

For this reason he had called in Kitai Ishibashi, the 'Suggestor,' who had the mental power to superimpose his own will on a person in such a manner that his subject remained convinced he was making his own decisions, completely unaware of being under a strange influence.

Bell perused the evaluations. The radio message from the sector where the two structure disturbances had been registered was a dilly.

'Slow as molasses,' Bell mumbled, figuring on the fingers of his hands that it took the message about 24 hours to reach the moon. 'And what's this?'

He studied the measurements of the angle at which the message had been beamed to the transceiver station on Luna. The calculations of Ron, the positronicomputer, were attached, confirming that the radio message in uncoded language stemmed from the ship which had caused the two structure disturbances 24 hours earlier.

'Looks as if we might be in for a humdinger,' Bell growled, speaking to nobody in particular, 'but who knows...?'

Commander Deringhouse was ready to report that everything was all clear at the controls of his new ship *Centurio* when the top alarm was sounded. Perry Rhodan's firm voice issued from the loudspeaker and soon he appeared on the picture screen. 'Commander Deringhouse! Take off at once! Hytrans to Pluto orbit. Locate the alien ship which leaped out of hyperspace yesterday. Be prepared for battle action! You'll receive immediately the computations of the position for your start and distance of transition. Repeat order, Commander Deringhouse!'

Deringhouse acknowledged the order word by word without hesitating. The airlocks of the *Centurio* closed.

Men and robots rushed to their posts on the ship's decks and the all-clear signals came in quick succession to the command center. Tension spread throughout the heavy cruiser.

With a whine the *Centurio* shot up into the sky. The huge sphere grew smaller and smaller, disappeared toward the bright sun and radioed back to Terrania from a height of 12 miles.

One hour later the second radio message came: 'Ready for hytrans. Deringhouse.'

All structure sensors in the solar system registered the disturbance when the *Centurio* jumped through hyperspace near Pluto's orbit.

Col. Freyt turned around briefly when he heard two men enter behind him and then no longer paid attention to Rhodan's and Khrest's presence.

'Another structure disturbance three minutes ago!' The information couldn't have been delivered more tersely but it was enough for Perry Rhodan. He didn't notice Khrest's admiring glance. The Arkonide was again impressed, as always, by Rhodan's method of concentrating only on the most crucial element of important matters. He was to be given another proof of this.

'The same ship, Freyt?'

'The brain's checking it out . . . Here comes the result, sir!'

They examined the read-out together: 'Probability 98.3% that same ship is involved which performed two transitions yesterday near Pluto orbit.'

'And how about the evaluation of the rangefinder?' Rhodan was anxious to know.

Col. Freyt was ready with the answer. 'The ship is coming from interstellar space and approaching the Solar system at 0.9% below velocity of light...'

The hypercom sounded and the *Centurio* came in: 'Alien ship spotted! Determined coördinates of position. Will make immediate approach. Deringhouse.'

The structure sensor of the *Centurio* had registered the transition of a spaceship in its vicinity. Commander Deringhouse glanced quickly at his radio officer. 'Hypercom Terrania,' he ordered and reported his message without realizing that Perry Rhodan listened in.

The *Centurio* soared away, leaving behind the coldly shining Solar planets. Pluto, circling the far distant Sun in eternal darkness, stood in opposition.

Commander Deringhouse was in his element. He sat serenely in his chair, his eyes glancing across the observation screens, switch panels and controls. As he regarded his officers he had the feeling of being in the best heavy cruiser in the solar system with the best crew.

'Position of the alien ship!' he demanded in a stern voice.

The positronic brain near the cartograph table started clicking and automatically delivered the data Deringhouse asked for. An officer submitted them quickly and precisely. 'Ten percent acceleration!'

The spherical spacer instantly leaped forward but the

sudden thrust went unnoticed inside the vessel. Not one unnecessary word was spoken.

The *Centurio* raced toward the strange spaceship with its gun turrets manned, waiting for the command to fire.

'Distance one light-minute!'

Deringhouse hesitated. The *Centurio* kept on course, racing toward the alien craft. All radio wave bands were closely watched for a message expected from the unknown spaceship.

'Distance 10 light-seconds!'

Deringhouse slowed down his ship to half speed. He wanted to avoid abrupt braking maneuvers as he approached the limit of safety.

'Distance 300,000 miles!'

'Clear gun flaps!' Deringhouse tersely ordered the turret gunners.

The distance reports followed each other closer and closer. Now they were no more than 25,000 miles away from their adversary.

'Damn Springers!' a man in the command center cried out. Deringhouse frowned but remained silent as he had just now had the same thought.

The Galactic traders were menacing a weak Earth. They had discovered the little planet in a minor arm of the Galaxy and believed they could mete out to it the same treatment they gave to many others of the inhabitated worlds in the Milky Way.

And now they rushed headlong toward one of the traders' ships, the mortal enemies of Terra.

'A message from the stranger!' a radio officer suddenly shouted, breaking Deringhouse's tension somewhat. 'Levtan asks permission to come aboard, Commander.'

Deringhouse leaned closer to the microphone. 'Attention, gun turrets! Use all weapons at the slightest suspicious move without waiting for command to fire!' He knew that he could depend on his men.

'Hypercom! Dunker, send a message to the Chief!' Deringhouse ordered calmly. 'Alien spaceship asks permission to send one of its members named Levtan aboard. Permission granted. I'm giving you our coödinates . . .'

Terrania simply confirmed the message, nothing else. 'Alien ship approaching us. Distance 5,000 miles!' the rangefinder section reported.

The safety limit had already been crossed. 'Let him come!' Deringhouse said, full of expectation.

Next to the mighty *Stardust II*, Perry Rhodan's battleship of half a mile diameter, stood the two heavy cruisers *Solar System* and *Terra*, ready to start.

Highest alert had been ordered for its crews by Terrania but neither Rhodan, Reginald Bell nor the two Arkonides were on board one of the spherical spaceships.

'Why do we sit around here and wait?' Thora asked impatiently. 'I don't know why you have to smirk, Reginald Bell!' she angrily snarled a moment later at Perry's friend who sat in a chair with a grin on his broad face.

'Because you're so excitable, Thora,' Reggie replied. 'I think you're getting downright human. Didn't you once call us Earth dwellers barbarians?'

Thora and Bell couldn't stand each other. They never let an opportunity pass to needle each other.

'I wonder why we hear nothing more from Deringhouse?' Khrest tried with his question to end the tiff between the two. 'It seems foolhardy to allow Levtan to come aboard the *Centurio*.'

'Deringhouse foolhardy, Khrest?' Perry smiled. 'But he ought to keep us informed.'

'Why don't we call him ourselves?' Thora insisted.

'All destroyers have been instructed to keep radio silence and I can't make an exception, Thora.'

'When did the Chief of the New Power renounce his special standing?' Thora asked tartly.

Perry was about to make a caustic riposte when he saw a pleading look in Khrest's eyes and so he only said: 'It's a distinction of the great to use self-control in small things, Thora, and prying is considered on Earth to be a vice.'

Throwing back her proud head, she walked out in a huff.

Khrest quickly apologized for her behaviour. 'She's so painfully disappointed that she can't go back to Arkon. Constantly waiting for the trip home, Perry; she's a woman. . . .'

'Alright, Khrest!' Perry hastened to change the subject as his conscience bothered him when it came to the topic of the Arkonides' return voyage. 'But why does the *Centurio* fail to call back?'

Rhodan looked out of the window to his spaceships. They were insignificant compared to the might of the Galactic traders and the Mounders.

A kingdom for an idea!

He, Perry Rhodan, was the most troubled and nervous man of the three in the room but he gave the appearance of an unshakable rock of calmness.

Why doesn't Deringhouse report again? he kept asking in his thoughts.

The hypercom remained silent.

Deringhouse bellowed into the microphone: 'Turret two, halt ship with warning shot before bow!'

A bright flash exploded on the vast panoramic screen in the command center. The *Centurio* demonstrated its power for the first time and almost blasted away the nose of the alien spacer at a distance of 2000 miles.

'We'll stop!' the second radio message came through. 'We've not come to attack you. We want to negotiate!'

Deringhouse thoughtfully gazed at his radio officer. There was something strange and disturbing in the message from the dealer's ship. In his opinion it sounded much too peace-loving.

'Commander to gun turrets!' he again called the battle stations. 'Strike at once if the Springer fails to stop in a minute!'

He switched over to call the radio officer. 'Send the same message to the other ship!'

'All of it' the radio officer asked.

'Yes, we want to let them know what they're up against.'

The tension in the command center kept growing. Deringhouse's eyes were riveted to the huge panoramic observation screen. The computer clacked as it reported the changes in distance. The message had been transmitted to the dealer Levtan.

'The alien ship stopped moving!'

The *Centurio* slowed down. The heavy cruiser flew in a wide curve around the other ship at a distance of 2000 miles.

'Their ship remains motionless!'

The *Centurio* accelerated again. Now it was exactly behind the ship at rest. Deringhouse exercised extreme caution, more than was called for in view of his ship's superior fighting power which exceeded that of the Springer a thousand times. He acted as if he were the weaker one.

Perhaps Khrest had told too many exaggerated stories about the clans and patriarchs of the traders. Or was the reason the difficulty in understanding why the Springers sought negotiations when they were already in the Solar system close to Earth and had only to reach out to strangle it in their iron fist?

Now the old instincts of the one-man pursuit pilot were aroused again in Deringhouse. The *Centurio* shot toward the strange ship. It quickly grew as a bright spot on the observation screen.

'A Springer . . .' somebody said in the command center.

'Heavens to Betsy!' Deringhouse exclaimed in surprise. 'What kind of a rusty bucket did the traders send us here'

At the same moment James Hugh called from his station: 'Foreign object, Commander. Body approaching at 67% below speed of light from Phi 3.65 and Theta 56.19!'

The positronicon had already registered these data and transmitted them to the gun turrets of the *Centurio.*

That was it! A simple trick of the traders – so simple that he had almost fallen for it. But why wasn't he given the report on the distance? How far away was the second ship?

With an incredible thrust of energy the *Centurio* shot in a tremendous leap past the rusty vessel, missing it by a hair. It performed a risky turning maneuver and raced toward the registered coördinates.

'Distance? What's keeping you?' Deringhouse inquired icily. 'Hugh, why don't you give me the distance?'

'The machine has submitted two different values,' Hugh replied meekly.

Deringhouse nearly jumped out of his seat. 'Then we'll have two more Springer ships against us! Both distances, Hugh! Hurry up!'

'4.38 and 4.71 light-seconds,' Hugh stammered out the information.

'We'll soon put a stop to that!' Deringhouse spoke in a deceivingly soft tone. 'And then we'll take care of Levtan, this treacherous angel of peace!'

Perry Rhodan looked up in dismay.

'What's the matter?' he asked angrily but indicated with a gesture of his hand that he was always willing to talk to John Marshall.

'The Ambassador of the Asian Federation requests an audience, Chief!'

'Send him to Bell, Marshall!' Perry quickly decided,

since he was unable and unwilling to spare a minute to listen to the jealousies between the power blocs of Terra.

'But the Ambassador insists on speaking to the Administrator of Terrania himself, Chief, and he refuses to be put off.'

'Nevertheless I'm denying his request. Tell him that as diplomatically as you can!' Thus Perry Rhodan put an end to the interruption. He contacted again the enormous communication center of the two million city of Terrania while John Marshall, the telepath, turned to leave.

'Nothing yet?' Rhodan asked impatiently.

'No, sir!' the speaker answered.

Rhodan instantly got in touch with the two heavy cruisers. '*Solar System* and *Terra* to take off at once. Take up positions for hypertrans to Pluto orbit. Order to leap follows separately!'

A moment later the roar of the powerful engines could be heard through the acoustic insulation of Rhodan's office as the spaceships started up. He turned his head and watched the heavy cruisers lift off and rush with increasing acceleration toward the high-flying clouds where they disappeared.

Rhodan was deeply worried and he breathed heavily. What had happened to the new *Centurio* beyond Pluto's orbit and what did the traders conspire to do? Was he – and with him the entire Earth – falling into a trap the Springers were about to spring? Had he failed to detect one of their ruses?

Once more he called the communication center. The

heavy cruiser *Centurio* and its Commander Deringhouse had not yet broken the silence.

'Two meteors!' Deringhouse exclaimed in disgust. They happened to be chunks of metal with magnetic fields. 'Back to that rusty bucket!'

He had lost valuable time. Now the *Centurio* had to show what it could do. The commander looked at his watch and was surprised to see how much time had elapsed meanwhile.

For a fleeting moment he wondered whether to call Terrania. He decided against it since there was nothing new to report.

He set his course again for the Springer ship which was still standing at the same spot.

It looked as if the *Centurio* was going to ram the alien spaceship with full force. More and more of the officers were casting anxious glances at Deringhouse with the same question in their eyes: *When will he brake?* Deringhouse flew the gigantic spacer like a one-man ship.

At the last moment the braking jets shrieked and the flight of the battleship was stopped in the grip of titanic fists. The G forces mounted steeply but the absorbers didn't let them rise above Value One. The crew of the ship didn't even feel the tremendous deceleration pressure.

Now the *Centurio* again accosted the rear of the Springer ship up to the border of its powerful defense screen, a silent, fearsome and haunting menace.

'Levtan may come aboard!' Deringhouse instructed his radio officer. 'But not in a vehicle, only in his spacesuit. Tell him we'll bring him safely aboard. Stress the word *safe.*'

The call went across and was confirmed by the Springers. Then they observed on the big panoramic view panel how a small airlock in the ship opened and a man in an Arkonide spacesuit firmly pushed himself away in the direction of the *Centurio.*

At this instant the radio transceiver picked up another message: '*Terra* and *Solar System* have just reported to Terrania that they've reached their positions in orbit of Pluto for a short hytrans maneuver.'

Quickly a magnetic beam from the *Centurio* seized the stranger in the spacesuit while the protective field of the heavy cruiser opened momentarily to haul the trader safely aboard.

Even now Deringhouse still thought that no new events had happened that should be reported to Rhodan but he couldn't get rid of the unpleasant feeling that he would be called down on the carpet by the chief after his landing.

Then came the word from the *Centurio's* entrance hatch. 'Man on board! Weapons search negative!'

'Escort him with four men and two fighter robots to the command center!' Deringhouse called back.

'It's a man seeking to negotiate after all,' James Hugh said but the undertone of his voice revealed that he failed to understand the meaning of what was going on and was filled with mistrust.

Deringhouse was also extremely suspicious and wary.

Chapter Three

THE STRATA METHOD

The *Centurio* and Levtan's 500-foot-long cylindrical ship had landed close together on the spaceport of Terrania. *Terra* and *Solar System* were once again stationed on the tarmac. Nothing indicated that their weapons of destruction were aimed at the *LEV XIV*. Rhodan had no intention of endangering Terrania by the deployment of his most devastating weapons.

The consultation on the situation had just come to an end. Bell looked incredulously at the delapidated ship of the trader. 'And Levtan looked just as disgusting on the screen,' he related his impression. 'It's quite some time since I've seen such a repugnant fellow!'

'And to think that because of this man our flight to Arkon was delayed!' Thora said pointedly disregarding Khrest's reproachful glances. Disdainfully she pursed her lips. 'This *LEV XIV* isn't and never has been a ship of the Springers!'

'We'll soon find out what the *LEV XIV* is and who has sent Levtan to us,' Rhodan quickly interjected, ending the discussion.

The stranger was brought to the door by Deringhouse

and two fighter robots. The slender man with distinctly mongoloid features straightened up when he saw the two fighter robots leave. With a supercilious grin he bowed briefly before the group of people awaiting him. He looked unkempt and neglected like his ship. The *LEV XIV* was not only rusted but also smelled to high heaven.

Thora turned up her nose at him and stepped back. Khrest studied the trader with scientific interest. Bell's broad face expressed everything a good diplomat is never supposed to show. Only Perry retained his usual composure and kept on top of the situation. He was not yet prepared to make a judgment as long as he didn't know what it was that had brought Levtan to Earth.

But it didn't take long to find out all about him as the best mutants who were assembled in the background began their task. John Marshall was already deeply probing Levtan's thoughts.

Khrest was the first to address the Springer. 'You're not a trader, Levtan! You *were* a trader. Now you're a *traitor!*'

A vicious look flashed briefly in Levtan's narrowed eyes. Then he looked up to the tall Arkonide. 'You're from Arkon?' he asked impudently instead of replying to Khrest's assertion.

'And you're a pariah!' Khrest reiterated his remark, admittting at the same time that he was indeed an Arkonide.

Perry Rhodan now received John Marshall's whispered advice: 'Levtan is a traitor and a desperate outcast. His thoughts are rife with insidious and vile intentions of blackmail. At present he's trying to figure out the most effective way to deceive us.'

Perry Rhodan stepped forward and told Levtan his name.

'Perry Rhodan!' the expelled Springer repeated, staring at the head of the New Power. 'Where is your second Arkonide battleship, Rhodan? I've always believed that it was nothing but a bluff. I know that the Arkonide empire has so far lost only one ship of this class but your secrets will be kept by me if we can do business together.'

Perry remained unperturbed. He kept his eyes coldly fixed on Levtan. 'I don't find it necessary to bluff . . .'

The insolence of the abominable Springer was amazing. Brazenly he interrupted Rhodan: 'I wouldn't admit each lie I've told either. You're lucky, Rhodan, that the Springer clans still believe you're in possession of two spacers of the *Stardust* class. Be that as it may . . .'

Now John Marshall came out of the background He walked past his chief and stopped in front of Levtan just short of stepping on his toes. Perry Rhodan considered it premature to teach Levtan manners and he whispered an order to Marshall to confront the Springer only with the facts.

John Marshall immediately bit his tongue and changed his line of approach. 'Levtan, you are planning to repeat the surreptitious plot by which you ruined the Gaxtek clan on the star Casters?'

Everybody in the room could hear how Levtan gasped for air. Then he uttered a gurgling groan and ducked like a dog that had been kicked. With a feral look in his eyes he asked Marshall, full of hate: 'What do you know about that?'

'Let's get to the point, Levtan!' Perry interjected in a tone which tolerated no contradiction. 'Why didn't you contact us via hypercom? Why did you use the slow frequency?' He purposely formulated his question carefully. Levtan's confidence had to be restored for the time being since the telepathic mutants had not yet extracted all information from him.

Levtan grinned arrogantly. 'I'm no fool. I didn't want to attract the Springers' attention by a hypercom message. Each of their ships monitors all communications ever since you appeared on the scene, Rhodan. Alright, let's talk business. I can sell you some crucial information. When I considered getting in touch with you, I first made sure that I'm protected. I'm not the only one who is an outcast. I have two friends who also know about your bluff of a second *Stardust* battleship and they're out there waiting for me to be back in 24 hours. Unless I return by that time they're prepared to take action. Now can we make a deal, Rhodan?'

Marshall whispered to Rhodan: 'It's only a trick of Levtan's but he thinks constantly about the traders and mainly about a meeting of great importance.'

Mention of a meeting greatly alarmed Perry Rhodan. 'Get to the bottom of this!' he gave Marshall to understand while Bell told Levtan: 'We know how to take care of you and your accomplices but we want to be peaceful, Springer. Anyway, don't try to tell us your story about your non-existent friends again. We ...'

But Levtan could not be intimidated so easily and Bell's threat fell flat. Slyly he examined the burly Reginald Bell. 'I made two transition jumps yesterday and one again today. The Galactic traders are not asleep. They probably have already taken the bearings of the structure disturbance and a fleet of the Mounders is perhaps now on the way . . .'

Now the telekineticist Tama Yokida who, by the power of his will, could move objects wherever he wanted, decided to get into the act. He willed Levtan to rise to the ceiling.

The pariah began to rise with horrified expressions slowly but surely toward the ceiling, wildly flailing his arms and trying to grab ahold of something.

'We ought to let you starve to death up there!' Bell growled, watching him intently. 'Levtan, you better tell what you have to offer us or we'll give you the same treatment as the Springers!'

Tama Yokida, the medium-sized stocky Japanese who had been a student of astronomy until Rhodan recognized his talents as a mutant and requested him to join his organisation, stood motionlessly in the background and kept the outcast Levtan floating near the ceiling.

Soon Marshall was able to inform his chief: 'He's weakening and has lost his desire to use his bag of tricks. He's not so sure anymore that his information has any value for us. Somewhere in the Galaxy an extraordinary meeting of the traders is going to take place . . .'

Perry Rhodan recognied that the stage had been set for him to take over the negotiations with the scurvy Springer. He passed the word through Marshall to the telekinetic Yokida to let Levtan come down again.

The terrified trader slowly descended like a balloon and stood on the floor. He wiped his bald head and stroked his sparse beard with his wet hand, sighing in anguish.

'Levtan,' Rhodan began calmly. 'You need help. You'll get all the assistance your ship needs. In turn we want you to tell us all you know about the meeting of the Galactic traders.'

It was a typical attribute of Perry Rhodan. He acted as if he had played his highest trump whereas he had only shown his lowest card.

'I need weapons,' Levtan rasped and his almond-shaped eyes glistened greedily.

At the same instant he screamed in fear and retreated toward the door. A man had taken form in front of him. A small slim man with the face of a child, appearing from nowhere. This man, a Japanese like Yokida, followed in Levtan's steps.

'I need weapons only as a last resort,' Levtan corrected himself quickly, obviously unwilling to make closer acquaintance with the slender man. 'By all the patriarchs! This is ghastly . . .'

'He's not leveling yet, Chief!' John Marshall whispered to Perry Rhodan

'Call on Ras Tschubai!' Rhodan ordered.

Levtan's fright exceeded all restraints. Just as he saw the little man take his last step toward him a second tall slender man with dark skin appeared out of thin air. 'My name is Ras Tschubai, Levtan! Shall I introduce my friends?'

'Chief, we've got him now where we want him,' Marshall informed Rhodan.

'Levtan,' Rhodan said in a tone pretending utter indifference, 'I give you one minute to sell me your bill of goods. If you're holding any part of it back I'll see to it that the Springers will be informed of your attempt . . .'

Suddenly Marshall interjected excitedly: 'Chief, Patriarch Etztak will give a report about *you* at the meeting of the Springers!' and Perry Rhodan with his customary presence of mind quietly added to his words to Levtan: 'Etztak will be highly pleased to drag you from the *LEV XIV*. Don't you think so?'

The pariah almost collapsed, barely managing to stay on his feet. He was glad to have the support of the black and the slight man at his left and right but when he reached out to lean on them he felt nothing and found himself standing alone near the door. The two had vanished in a flash; dissolved into nothing. In the same moment he saw them quietly standing together at a window behind a group of people in the room.

'I . . . I . . .' he panted and staggered, pressing his hands against his temples, 'I'll . . . tell you everything. I don't want to make a deal . . .'

'Then let's have it!' Perry Rhodan said tersely, reinforcing his words with a stern look.

The *LEV XIV* was refurbished on Terrania like a new ship. Perry Rhodan put 300 robots to work on the battered craft and showed such generosity toward Levtan that Bell was consternated and muttered disgustedly: 'You don't have to stuff millions down the throat of this traitor by force, Perry!'

Rhodan looked thoughtfully at his friend. 'Remember when I was ready to give a kingdom for an idea?'

'So what? Are you trying to tell me that this brigand of the stars has provided you with such an idea with his treason? Perhaps you want to conquer the planet where the patriarchs gather to plot our destruction?'

'Yes!'

'A kingdom for a chair!' Bell gasped with a futile look. 'Perry, you're playing as bad a joke as *It* when we were shown a cold shoulder and denied admittance through the protective screen of Wanderer. Conquer a planet? With what? Our tiny fleet against the Springers?'

'Maybe there're better ways of conquering a planet than trying to attack it with a space armada,' Rhodan replied undauntedly, smiling at Reginald Bell and stepping aside to greet Kitai Ishibashi.

Disconcertedly Bell gazed at his friend. It was true that Perry was ready to give a kingdom for an idea but now he was throwing away millions for that roving gipsy. A kingdom is expensive! Blast it, how did he expect to tackle the patriarchs without using the fleet?

He saw Perry and Kitai Ishibashi, the Suggestor, huddle together but Bell didn't figure out what they were up to.

The alert was cancelled. Rhodan's highest aides pleaded with him not to run such a risk. He refused and remained silent on the subject even to Bell. But Reginald knew his friend well and sensed that Perry was forcing an idea to take shape.

Rhodan went to visit Khrest. They chattered together and the Head of the New Power ostensibly acted as though there existed no danger at all from the Galactic traders.

When Rhodan ended the conversation Khrest was under the impression of having spent a rare leisurely hour in pleasant conversation with the usually preoccupied Perry.

On his way to Dr. Frank Haggard, the discoverer of the anti-leukemia serum which saved Khrest's life after his Arkonide spaceship crash-landed on the Moon, Rhodan ran into Bell.

'Where are you going, Perry?'

'To see Dr. Haggard.'

'And where have you been?'

'Oh, with Khrest.'

'Seems you're in a hurry, Perry! I'm too.'

With amusement Perry watched his burly friend leave. He knew what bothered Bell: he was still trying to guess what action he had in mind to protect the imperilled Earth. Now Reggie was on his way to sound out Khrest for some clues.

Dr. Haggard was also surprised to see Perry Rhodan in such high spirits and didn't notice anything unusual when Bell came to inquire about the purpose of the visit. He willingly told him all about their conversation.

Bell went back to his office in a disgruntled mood. He had not been able to find out anything tangible and when the Chief held a conference with the mutants he didn't attach any special importance to it. Routine consultation, he thought.

However in this conference Perry Rhodan's plan had already taken on definite form.

Kitai Ishibashi unobtrusively wiped the perspiration from his brow. The tall, haggard Japanese suggestor looked completely exhausted. He had faced a formidable task and just accomplished it: Kitai Ishibashi had succeeded in impressing his will so indelibly on the crew of 40 men of the *LEV XIV*, including the wily Levtan, that they now believed they exercised each act and thought and made all statements according to their own free will.

He had implanted a mass of data in their minds, installing them furtively like a complicated maze of gears and now Perry Rhodan had conducted a gruelling test of Levtan in his presence. Everything had functioned smoothly.

'Thank you, Ishibashi,' Perry Rhodan said warmly, shaking the hand of the Japanese, 'but this was not the last job for you.'

His ingenious plan, which later became known as Galactic Interception in the chronicles of mankind, had more than one aspect.

Everything fell in place with the precision of a structure sensor. Bell suddenly missed the teleporter Tako Kakuta. Before he inquired about him, he became aware that he had seen neither John Marshall nor Tama Yokida in a few days.

'Where are they?' he bellowed into the telecom. 'Did

I understand you right? Kakuta, Marshall and Yokida are all in the sickbay? In Haggard's private section?'

And that's where they were, indeed, as Reginald Bell found out when he sought them out at once. Dr. Haggard led him to three beds. Bell was baffled, looked again and growled at the physician: 'I came to see our mutants, not these gypsies from the stars.'

'But these *are* our mutants,' Dr. Haggard explained patiently.

Bell had one of his grouchy days. 'Dr. Haggard!' he said sharply at the moment when one of the three beds was suddenly empty and the patient materalized close to Bell.

Bell swallowed hard. 'Kakuta!' he shouted and tried to grab the slight Japanese who now looked like a member of Levtan's crew. However his brawny hands gripped nothing but empty air. Tako Kakuta had teleported himself in a second tiny jump back to bed.

'I'm sick, sir!' Kakuta exclaimed, grinning all over his face. The little man who had pulled many such pranks on Bell was also cautious. He knew the temper of the other.

'Some day I'll wring your neck!' Bell hissed. He gave Dr. Haggard a grim look and stomped out.

Slowly it began to dawn on him. He divined Perry's plan and didn't think too much of it. On the corridor outside the private section of the sickbay he murmured: 'It's a desperate clutch at the famous straw!'

Reginald Bell had been sent as Rhodan's emmissary to Peking. The Asiatic Federation believed it had reasons for complaining about transgressions of the western power bloc.

He had been detained for three days by meetings and conferences with the Asian Federation and for three days he had been annoyed by the bagatelles which were of inconsequential proportions compared to the peril threatening Terra as a whole. But the western power bloc had not been entirely blameless in the discord with the Asiatic Federation.

Bell had conducted his talks in Peking with the voice of an angel. On the evening of the third day, however, when he realized after interminable consultations that he had made not one iota of progress, his patience was exhausted.

Perry Rhodan couldn't have sent a more undiplomatic emissary to Peking than Reginald Bell! But Bell's methods seemed to bring results. When he called Washington from the conference room and talked in no uncertain language, he was finally able to drop into bed at midnight, muttering to himself: 'At last!'

He flew back to Terrania in a pursuit ship. He piloted it himself. It was a pleasure of which he never let himself be deprived. The commander of the craft sat next to him in the co-pilot's seat.

Bell was in the best frame of mind. The commander of the craft broke out in a cold sweat and had trouble catching his breath. He pictured his craft lying smashed on the ground as Bell plummeted in a reckless steep curve down to the edge of the spaceport.

'Sir!'

'Why, what's bothering you?' Bell asked with a grin on his broad face, taking time out to look at his co-pilot.

Then, all of a sudden, the immense braking forces of the pursuit ship pulled the craft out of its course. Bell moved in a horizontal direction and the ship touched the ground with a hardly noticeable tap.

'Back home again,' Bell said, looking over the spaceport. He had already forgotten that he had nearly scared his co-pilot to death with his stunning maneuver. Suddenly he leaned forward and stared at the landing pads of the heavy spaceships.

Stardust II was missing! The half-mile big spherical battleship of Perry Rhodan was nowhere to be seen!

'Where is Rhodan?' he yelled into the microphone.

'On Venus,' the answer came from the loudspeaker.

Using the positronic brain on Venus was the only way to evaluate the chances of success Perry Rhodan's plan could have.

The positronic brain had been installed by the Arkonides on Venus inside a rock many thousands of years ago and then forgotten in the course of time until Rhodan had rediscovered it. He used it frequently.

Now he stood once again alone in front of its huge control panel and fed almost endless sequences of data into the mammoth mechanical brain.

On the flight to Venus he had talked for hours to Khrest about the Galactic traders, their clans, laws and customs.

Soon the positronic brain informed him that he would be furnished the result in 24 hours. Patiently he settled down to wait. As he quietly relaxed in the room before 'Ron,' he contemplated the traders and the potentially greatest danger Terra had faced.

The race was as old as the Arkonides but had developed between the stars into a race of their own and adopted laws to maintain their identity and a loose unity.

The ancient code stipulated that an exiled member of clan could only be reinstated if he performed an extraordinary deed from which the whole race of the traders drew a rich benefit.

Finally the brain furnished the sought for answer to the problem. Perry's hands trembled when he read the exact evaluation and realized that new problems had to be mastered in addition to the given solutions.

One hour later he returned with the *Stardust* to Earth. He arrived 30 minutes after Bell had come back to Terrania from Peking.

Kitai Ishibashi, the suggestor, called the procedure he used Strata Method.

Perry Rhodan interrupted him: 'Ishibashi, I can't take chances. The risk is too great. This time I must depend solely on your ability. You'll have to put not only Levtan into a state of deep suggestion but the same treatment must be applied to each member of his crew. Is that clear?'

'Certainly, sir!'

'Come with me. Levtan is waiting in the next room. I've asked him to come for a session with me.'

Kitai Ishibashi's suggestive powers penetrated deeper

and deeper into Levtan while Rhodan watched them both.

The Suggestor imbedded his will in the dispelled trader in stratas. Earlier he had mentioned transplantation to Perry Rhodan, the method of grafting healthy skin to large section of a burned body.

Ishibashi's mind and imaginative powers were transformed in Levtan's consciousness as his own experience and knowledge. They lost their extraneous quality and became one with the pariah.

Levtan saw in his mind Rhodan's fortifications on Venus with their vast caverns hidden in mountains and excavations stretching for hundreds of miles, the gigantic spaceship-manufacturing plants and factories pouring out incredible numbers of fighter robots and weapons on their conveyors.

And Kitai Ishibashi's imagery conjured up pictures of gigantic Venusian spaceports, sunk deep below the surface of the soil and protected by defense screens and immense gates behind miles of rock, holding more than 100 cruisers of the *Terra* and *Solar System* class as well as 22 spherical spacers, looking exactly like *Stardust II*.

Perry studied Kitai Ishibashi closely. The mutant seemed to be asleep. He sat in his chair, leaning slightly with hands folded and eyes closed. No sign in his face indicated the enormous effort with which he labored.

Eventually Ishibashi opened his eyes and gave Rhodan at the same time a hint that it was now his turn as Head of the New Power to take over Levtan's guidance.

Perry glanced at his watch. Only a minute had elapsed since Ishibashi had started the treatment of the Springer who now woke up from his state of suggestion and answered the last question he had heard from Rhodan before the 'treatment.'

'Yes,' the Head of the New Power replied quietly. 'You can start in three days, Levtan. I believe we've worked out a good deal together, don't you?'

Perry Rhodan knew exactly what Levtan saw in his mind. The outcast of the Springers saw in a figment of his imagination the fortress on Venus, more than a hundred cruisers and 22 spherical battleships a half mile big – an armada in fighting trim.

He contrasted the value of this information with the importance of his own treachery and decided to agree with Rhodan's question. However even now his cunning nature came to the fore again. 'But you've also gained other advantages, Perry Rhodan. Your robots have spied in every nook and cranny of my ship. I bet you've found many things on board which were new to you.'

'You still have too high an opinion of yourself, Levtan. Megalomania is the last step down the road of disaster.'

'It's easy for you to talk with your 22 ships of the *Stardust* class,' Levtan said acrimoniously, plain envy in his eyes, but in the next moment he was again the smooth-talking operator versed in every trick of the trade. 'Well, anyway I got out of a jam. You said I may leave in three days?'

'You *must* leave, Levtan. Your four sick men have recovered and will be discharged from the hospital today.'

'Tomorrow, sir!' Kitai Ishibashi interjected. He felt so exhausted that he was unwilling to go through another session like this the same day. He knew that it would disturb Rhodan's time plan and felt relieved when Rhodan quickly corrected himself.

'I get it,' Levtan replied with a stealthy look. 'I'm being thrown out! That's about what I had expected on Earth!'

Dr. Frank Haggard summoned the entire crew of the *LEV XIV* for an examination in the dispensary. Only Levtan was excused – he had already received his treatment.

One of the clan grumbled about the vaccinations: 'What are these shots for?'

Haggard gave him a little lecture. Each shot lasted a minute. This was enough time for Kitai Ishibashi to apply his Strata Method.

Ishibashi himself became the last patient. So far he had no resemblance to one of the roving star gypsies. Calmly he laid down on the operating table and placed himself in the capable hands of Dr. Haggard and his Arkonide medical science. He had already made sure that nobody on the *LEV XIV* would give it another thought when the fourth of the patients would leave the hospital one day later and return to the ship.

The last thing Kitai Ishibashi heard before the anesthesia took full effect was the sound of music from an unreal world.

Chapter Four

TO GOSZUL'S PLANET

Three weeks after its landing on Earth the *LEV XIV* lifted off the Terranian spaceport again and ascended slowly into the cloudless sky over the Gobi Desert.

Levtan the Springer, who had been expelled from the community of clans of the Galactic traders, now left Earth with a crew increased by four men to betray Perry Rhodan!

The Galactic Interception was in full swing!

As the *LEV XIV* grew smaller in the distance the protective screen around the city of Terrania with its two million inhabitants closed up again and there was not the slightest hint pointing to an alarm until Rhodan called for it.

Take-off time was announced in the command centers of his four super-battleships. Blastoff in two hours!

Seldom had the speculation about the destination of their flight been so unsubstantiated as today. 'Proceed to Pluto's orbit!' were Rhodan's instructions.

This was the same course Levtan's ship had taken. Did Perry Rhodan want to follow the pariah from a safe distance to find out where the *LEV XIV* was heading? Did he, in the final analysis, mistrust the knowledge his telepaths had gleaned from the recesses of Levtan's brain and did he after all have doubts about the impending conclave of the patriarchs in system 221-Tatlira?

221-Tatlira. No system was listed under this name in the extensive star catalog of *Stardust II*. However they had found its reference data in the catalog of *LEV XIV*.

At take-off Perry Rhodan manned the controls of the *Stardust* himself and the *Centurio*, the *Terra* and the *Solar System* followed in its wake. The speed was kept lower than light. There was an air of tension in the ships. Nobody was accustomed to such crawling.

Four men of the Mutant Corps were missing: John Marshall, the telepath; the teleporter Tako Kakuta; Kitai Ishibashi, the suggestor; and the reticent Tama Yokida, who was never suspected by the uninitiated to be a telekineticist with improbable capabilities.

Perry Rhodan didn't allow the question concerning their whereabouts to be broached. He had become a pole radiating calmness all around him. Only one person didn't believe in his inner calm: Reginald Bell. But he kept silent.

Feverish excitement simmered inside Rhodan and he resembled a volcano close to eruption, the Chief of the New Power was now embarked on his greatest and most dangerous enterprise. During Earth's history its fate had never hung on such a thin thread!

The rangefinders of the *Stardust* kept a close check on the mercantile ship. Rhodan's four ships came to a stop near Pluto's orbit and remained motionlessly suspended in space. 'We'll be waiting here,' Rhodan declared laconically.

He stood in front of the big positronicomputer and glanced thoughtfully now and then at Ron's expansive control panel. Everyone gave the boss a wide berth, Bell included.

Something was definitely in the air – or was Rhodan only waiting for the transition of the trading ship to take place?

Suddenly the structure sensor registered a hytrans jump and Rhodan quickly demanded all data. When he received them he submitted them to the positronicomputer at once. Bell and the others watched him work. They were at a loss to understand Rhodan's hasty but nonetheless most precise efforts.

Rhodan switched a lever connecting the computer of the *Stardust* with those on board the three other cruisers. When the result was emitted it was simultaneously received on the *Terra*, the *Solar System* and the *Centurio*.

'Hytrans in three seconds!' Rhodan snapped into the mike.

The count atomatically began on all four ships. The mechanical computer Ron performed thousands of switching operations on each ship and they leaped as a coördinated group into hyperspace at the same instant.

Under an incredible discharge of energy the mighty spherical ships left the normal universe through hyperspace and zero-time, phenomenons which still defied man's comprehension, and were hurled across enormous distances, materializing again in the familiar space-time continuum.

As always Perry Rhodan was the first to awake from the twilight zone of impaired consciousness and to shake off the shock of transition. He immediately checked the most important instruments while the others slowly returned to reality.

'Sun-like system. Distance 1012 light-years from Earth. Seven planets. One of them, the second closest is Goszul's Planet according to the catalog of the Springers.' Perry Rhodan pointed to the huge panoramic screen of the *Stardust* where one star outshone all other suns.

He noticed Bell's questioning look.

'Object spotted!' an excited voice sounded at this moment.

Rhodan turned calmly to the officer at the rangefinder. 'If it's only a single object, it must be the *LEV XIV*. Levtan is on his way to Goszul's Planet to reveal the strength of our battle fleet to the patriarchs of the trader clans. Is it only one body?'

'That's all, sir!' the man stuttered, overwhelmed by Rhodan's certainty. 'It's moving at 150,000 miles per second toward the second planet. But . . .'

'But what?' Rhodan asked curtly.

'What about our transition jump, sir? The Springers must have picked up the space disturbance caused by us!'

Perry Rhodan walked over and stood behind him, putting his hand on his shoulder. He said with a force that was almost hypnotic: 'The *LEV XIV* had to traverse the distance of over 100 light-years in two jumps. The second jump of the *LEV XIV* and our own jump coincided. If we're lucky the traders have noticed only one transition and when they see the pariah, they'll assume that he came alone!'

Luck was with them.

Chapter Five

HUMAN TIME BOMB

Levtan shuddered when he recognised the flaming star 221-Tatlira after he had pulled out of the shock of the second transtition. He was gripped by panic and fear of the patriarchs leading the Galactic traders because he had been banned from their society when they accused him of being a scoundrel.

He approached the second planet at 80% of the speed of light, turning a deaf ear to the members of his clan. With a distorted face he kept staring at his instruments. He didn't know whether he was flying to his death or into a new life of acceptance in the community of the traders.

'Leave me alone!' he barked at his nephew who sat in the seat of the co-pilot. 'I'm flying the ship! This is *my* ship and I'm the Commander!'

His shouting could be heard three doors away. Adjacent to the command center a luxurious room was occupied by seven men. The room was equipped with all the comforts owing to the generosity of Perry Rhodan. His mutants had chosen it for themselves and Kitai Ishibashi had no trouble suggesting to Levtan that he offer it to them.

Unobtrusively they exchanged glances. 'The old man is

slowly coming unglued,' John Marshall commented lazily, fiddling with the fine adjustment control of his picture screen.

'I hope we can pull it off,' Kakuta worried. He had discovered a few points on the observation screen which had not been present a few seconds before.

'Here they come!' they heard Levtan bellow in the command center.

'I count six of them,' Tako Kakuta stated.

They made no comment but Levtan shouted: 'A battleship, a battleship!'

The amplifiers on the *LEV XIV* were turned up to the highest volume and everybody on board could hear in the farthest corners the query from the battleship: 'Please identify your ship by number and clan!'

Levtan was swamped by a new wave of panic. Instead of replying and stating the purpose of his flight, he veered from his course to port and accelerated to maximum velocity.

A brilliant beam flashed from the depth of space aiming savagely at the *LEV XIV*. But it was a lucky hour in the stars for the pariah and he was thankful that his abrupt change of course had saved him and his ship from being turned into a cloud of gas.

The next shot from the battleship also went wild. Levtan turned his ship upside down, twisting and dodging. The seven men in the cabin next to the command center held their breath. They saw the sun 221-Tatlira swirl across the observation screen and disappear at the upper border.

'Let me see how bad the weather is,' John Marshall said and got up.

'Bundle yourself up!' warned Dorget, one of the clan.

'I want to go with you,' Kitai Ishibashi spoke up, walking around two men and slipping into the corridor with Marshall.

They looked at each other. Nobody in his right mind could have foreseen such an incident, not even Perry Rhodan.

Suddenly the protective screens of the *LEV XIV* were caught in a devastating beam from the battleship. For a split second the energy for the ship's gravity regulator was cut off and every man in the spacer felt as thought he were breaking apart under the enormous pressures.

The danger point passed but two of the three protective fields of the mercantile spacer were knocked out of operation. The curses in the engine room became strong and audible.

'Levtan is crazed by fear. He no longer knows what he's doing,' Marshall told the Suggestor and tried to tune in again immediately on the treacherous Springer's thoughts.

Kitai Ishibashi wondered whether the fault could be his. Perhaps he had failed to keep Levtan long enough in the state of deep suggestion.

'I must go to the command center,' Marshall whispered to his comrade, jumping out of Levtan's nephew's way as he came cursing out of the command center and stormed down the corridor to the engine room.

The hatch door to the command center had not yet moved back again when John Marshall entered. Nobody paid attention to him as they all stared at the observation screen. There were four men present in the room besides Levtan.

Marshall realized that the mind of the desperate captain was filled with pure panic and a mad whirl of disconnected thought fragments. If Kitai Ishibashi didn't intervene at once with his special powers, the *LEV XIV* could disintegrate any minute.

New flashes blinked in three spots on the screen as the other destroyers jumped into the fray. They were far superior to Levtan's ship in every respect.

Suddenly one of Levtan's closest relatives leaped forward, pulled him out of his seat and yelled into his twisted face: 'You damn coward! Why don't you tell them who we are and why we came? Do you want us to be blown up, you fool?'

A blinding light burst on the screen and blotted out John Marshall's sight. Luckily it was no direct hit, only a ray in close proximity.

'Start talking!' the man kept yelling at Levtan and grabbed his head with both hands, pushing him in front of the hypercom microphone. 'Tell 'em!'

Marshall heard Perry Rhodan's name mentioned and that he talked about the base on Venus and the terrific fleet of heavy cruisers as well as the 22 super-battleships of the *Stardust* class.

Outside the hatch of the command center stood Kitai Ishibashi. He seemed to dream. Not a muscle in his face indicated that he intervened with his power in the struggle which threatened them with instant death. His tremendous suggestive forces leaped across 25,000 miles, penetrated the protective screen of the space battleship and bored into the brain of its commander.

Kitai Ishibashi didn't know that Levtan had already mentioned Perry Rhodan's name in his stammering. He was surprised to see how easy it was to influence the Commander. He virtually could feel it in his body that his mental defenses waned and that he almost eagerly absorbed the ideas he suggested to him.

Relentlessly he pounded into the mind of the battleship's commander to give his instructions to the other destroyers to cease their attacks.

Again Kitai Ishibashi applied his Strata Method. Though this procedure somewhat delayed the effect, it had the advantage that the layers, once they were built up homogeneously, were not felt as a foreign intrusion. The Commander genuinely believed he acted without coercion when he passed his orders to the destroyers via telecom: 'Cease attack! Escort Levtan and wait for permission to land!'

Levtan's scream from the command center woke Kitai Ishibashi from his dream state. He breathed heavily, rubbed his eyes and walked in a stooped gait back to his cabin.

'Well,' the teleporter Kakuta greeted him. 'How's the weather?'

Blandly, as if he had indeed checked it, Kitai Ishibashi replied: 'It's better now but it won't last long.'

The skirmish between the ships of the traders had taken

place far from the *Stardust* and the three cruisers, too distant to be seen on their huge picture screens. However the distance didn't exceed the range of their sensitive measuring instruments and the needles deflected wildly each time a disintegrator beam was shot at the *LEV XIV*.

Deadly silence reigned in the command center of the *Stardust*. Perry Rhodan stood like a statue before the big panel and watched the array of instruments.

'Why doesn't Kitai Ishibashi lift a hand?' he asked with utter dismay. What could have brought on Levtan's absurd and frantic behaviour and how could he have been so stupid as to refuse to identify his ship when the battleship of the Springers challenged him?

Then they recognised Levtan's voice and his babbling on the hypercom.

'That miserable wretch!' Bell thundered.

The cowardice of the pariah threatened the debacle of Perry Rhodan's Galactic Interception and imperilled the life of his four best mutants.

Five more disintegrator beams lunged ferociously at the *LEV XIV*. Perry held his breath involuntarily as he kept his eyes glued to three instruments set close together. Would the next deflection be even stronger and show that the *LEV XIV* was dissolved into a cloud of gas?

Again the hypercom registered a call: 'Cease attack! Escort Levtan and wait for permission to land!'

Somebody in the command center was muttering: 'And after the landing they're going to break down our mutants and make mincemeat out of them!'

Perry Rhodan whirled around to the speaker. The young

officer who had made the remark was bent with reddened face over his console.

Rhodan became aware that he had not even informed Bell about his plan. 'Our mutants won't be broken down,' he explained quietly and his grey eyes twinkled a little. 'The crew of the *LEV XIV* is under the constraint of suggestion and is cognizant of the fact that they have four more men on board. You may rest assured that our men look just like their own gang.'

The observer reported: 'Flotilla with *LEV XIV* on course to second planet!' But now the nerve-wracking tension in the command center of the *Stardust* had subsided.

Khrest, who had remained unobtrusively in the background, gave admiring credit to the man who took his place in the pilot seat of the *Stardust*—Perry Rhodan, the Peacelord of the Universe.

With greatly reduced speed the destroyer formation of the Springers with the *LEV XIV* in its midst glided at low altitude over Goszul's Planet.

The world bore the name of the trader Goszul who had discovered and conquered it. Rhodan's mutants were amazed to see lovely landscapes and a vast industrial center on the observation screen. Even the genuine clansmen made no secret of their surprise.

'So this is where they have their plants,' said Dorget. He was perturbed and scratched his bald skull.

Marshall appeared to contemplate his own thoughts. He had an absent look while he strained to recognize the thoughts of the pariahs. However, their knowledge of Goszul's Planet was based only on rumors. Levtan had been purged from the community of the Springers many years ago and at that time life on the planet had been a peaceful idyll.

The destroyer formation returned in a wide curve to the impressive production center. It seemed that the *LEV XIV* had been granted permission to land.

The ship had barely touched down when Levtan's order went to all cabins: 'Get ready to leave the ship!'

The mutants let the three real clansmen go first and hesitated to leave.

'We'll be arrested,' Marshall informed them. Their faces betrayed no astonishment. They had expected as much.

Tama Yokida the Telekin glanced at the cache of formidable hand weapons hidden by Rhodan's robots in the cabin. John Marshall's face blanched a shade. Again he probed some thoughts and returned to reality. 'We can't take it along,' he decided. 'Each one leaving the ship will be searched . . .'

'Also with . . .'

Marshall had already understood Ishibashi's thought, 'Yes, that too. We'll be spared for the time being only one thing: they won't put our brains through the wringer. The Springers trust Levtan no farther than they can throw him and I can't blame them for it. But now we must leave. We're the last ones'

Goszul, the discoverer of system 221-Tatlira and conqueror of the second planet – patriarch Goszul – still enjoyed the best of health. He was listening to the news about the landing of the *LEV XIV*.

Three other patriarchs sat in comfortable armchairs at a round table and listened attentively to the reports. The name Perry Rhodan had been mentioned repeatedly and each time a patriarch's face expressed hate while breathing heavily.

Etztak's breathing of vengeance had not escaped the sturdy old bald-headed Goszul. 'Don't you approve of Levtan's landing or does the name of Rhodan arouse your ire?' The wily Goszul gazed with a piercing look at his friend who had once believed he could wipe out Rhodan and considered himself lucky to be the only one to have eluded the Earthling in the attempt.

'I don't like either one,' Etztak replied with amazing calm. 'I know Levtan. He's a coward and nothing but a cunning criminal.'

'And what about Perry Rhodan? Why don't you say anything about him? I'd be interested to hear your opinion of him, Etztak.'

Etztak looked warily at Goszul. The other two patriarchs sensed the beginning of a sharp dispute and one of them interjected hastily: 'Wouldn't it be better to wait first for disclosures from Levtan's interrogation? After that we still can discuss this Perry Rhodan.'

Etztak's voice hissed: 'Not *this* Perry Rhodan, it's *The* Perry Rhodan who has found the World of the Immortal and knows how to get there! You can't deprecate such a man with a word like "this".'

The bald-headed patriarch Goszul grinned craftily. 'You talk the way it suits you at the moment, Etztak. I've never believed that fairy tale about the World of Eternal Life. Let's end this useless conversation. We don't have much time. The conference is scheduled to begin in two hours and I have to attend another meeting before we can set the final program for the Great Conclave.'

Perry Rhodan's mutants stood in the big airlock of the *LEV XIV* and watched as one after another of the crew members passed inspection by the traders and were put on a vehicle under guard.

'That doesn't augur very well for us,' Tako Kakuta stated.

At this moment a trader barked at them 'Do you want me to send you a special invitation?'

Kitai Ishibashi went first. Calmly he let them search him for weapons. Then he was taken between two heavily armed traders to a vehicle to be driven away. 'If you make one false move,' he was threatened, 'we'll shoot!'

He listened without saying a word. When he had taken a seat in the vehicle with a guard, the car remained immobilized.

'Why don't you get going?' the guard shouted at the driver who didn't move a finger to get started.

'I'm supposed to wait for the three last men to get on,' the young Springer replied quietly and registered no surprise when the loudmouth suddenly said agreeably: 'That's right, we were told to wait for these traitors.'

Kitai Ishibashi smiled inwardly. He was happy with

what he had accomplished. It was a great comfort to know his friends were near him.

Etztak held a consultation with his clan.

'Keep your eyes and ears open tomorrow when Levtan is questioned before the Great Conclave. Don't forget that Rhodan has almost succeeded in our downfall. So far I've been unable to make Goszul understand how dangerous Rhodan is . . .'

His son interrupted him. The interruption was a gross violation of their customs but Etztak let it pass. 'When you talk about Levtan, do you also mean Rhodan?'

'Haven't I made this clear,' the patriarch scowled at his son. 'Levtan claims to have escaped from Rhodan's armament center. I know how difficult it is to elude his grip. I don't believe Levtan. He has always been false and I fear that he wants to betray us to Rhodan.'

'Do you believe Levtan's assertions that Rhodan has 22 super-battleships . . .?'

'If you interrupt me once more I'll make you clean a whole deck,' Etztak bellowed at his son. 'No! I don't want to hear any more stupid questions! No, I don't believe Levtan's stories. Rhodan has only two of the large ships, not 22, and neither does he have 100 cruisers. Rhodan has bought the pariah and is now trying to find out what we're planning to do about his meddling in our affairs. He knows his weakness . . .'

At the risk of being punished by being made to clean the biggest deck on his knees, his son broke in for the third time: 'Father, do you call it weakness the way Rhodan has smashed our fleet?'

Etztak was in an uproar but reason prevailed over the old man's wrath. His son had reminded him of a debacle from which he had suffered nightmares for four months, waking up bathed in sweat.

Reluctantly he replied: 'I've tried to tell Goszul again that Perry Rhodan was on the World of Eternal Life and that he has there obtained the mysterious weapon with which he can make ships simply disappear. But Goszul refuses to admit it. He thinks these rumors are only wild imagination.'

'Or he is loath to realize that Perry Rhodan must be considered a peril of the highest magnitude?' his son ventured to say again. 'I don't think that Goszul has ever had to taste defeat.'

To everyone's surprise Etztak nodded condescendingly to his son and remarked: 'I've often quietly wished that Goszul would get into a confrontation with Rhodan. One would be enough to make him think and talk differently. Now you and you and you,' he pointed at three men, 'will take part tomorrow at the Great Conclave as observers. You must be vigilant when Levtan makes his statements; he'll be required to show proof. Remember that he comes from Rhodan and never forget what Rhodan did to our ships!'

The four mutants had made careful mental notes of every detail as they drove by on their way to the prison in a fortress. The heavy artillery emplacement on the grounds bristled with guns similar to those of the *Stardust II* and their cruisers. The Galactic traders had built unassailable fortifications, strong enough to withstand any onslaught from space.

The longer the ride, the clearer it became to the mutants how enormous and insurmountable the task was they faced here.

There were installations for every purpose and of many types; spaceship assembly plants, huge factories and thousands of robots for the variety of jobs. There were also masses of people with a reddish skin. They looked strangely like humans and made a very appealing impression.

These lazy Goszuls ...

This was the only reference John Marshall was able to deduce from the minds of the Springers about the short red-skinned people with remarkably rich dark hair. They were called Goszuls by their masters, who despised them.

After they entered the fortress the four mutants crossed a field divided in three sectors by two high wall systems secured by a curtain of rays as was quite obvious from the antennas on their ridges.

John Marshall uttered his first remark to his guard. It was derisive and full of defiance. 'You traders seem to have plenty of black sheep among yourselves! This prison is for monsters!'

The guard on his left snapped viciously: 'Take my advice, you scum, and don't open your trap in the future! You'll find out who's locked up in there ...' And he thought about the lazy mob of Goszuls who stubbornly resisted the hypno-training and remained devious and treacherous in spite of their efforts.

The vehicles stopped moving and set down in a row.

'Get out!' they were ordered.

A screen of protective rays was deactivated. A guard stepped out of a gate and asked gruffly: 'Are these really the last of the traitors?'

This was the name pinned on Levtan's people the minute they set foot on Goszul's planet.

The escorts were glad to get rid of their prisoners and one of them answered with annoyance: 'What reason do you have to bellyache? I'd like to get a lazy job like yours. Sign the papers, take the prisoners away and get out of my sight!'

The mutants looked at each other. This was noticed by a Springer and he kicked Tako Kakuta, hurling the slight Japenese against the gate sentry. The latter jumped to the side with a curse at the last moment and shouted at the Springer: 'You idiot! You almost caused an accident. I'm going to report you and you can bet that they'll come looking for you before night!'

John Marshall followed his thoughts but he also recognized what Tako Kakuta was up to. Tako took his time getting back on his feet. Now he stood behind the sentry.

'Get in!' the sentry growled at the others. They passed through and the guard signed the receipt for Levtan's men. The brutal trader took the receipt and turned to get back into the car. The sentry gave him a last disgusted look and was about to lead his new prisoners away when he heard a scream.

John Marshall gulped and glanced furtively at Tako Kakuta. The Japanese had disappeared for a fraction of a second in a short teleport jump to retaliate against the cruel trader in kind, then quickly leaped back and stood again at the spot where he had been before in the hallway.

Cursing wildly the trader picked himself up, holding his forehead. He had struck hard against a metal edge in his fall.

'You kicked me!" he screamed at the sentry in a blind rage.

'I kicked you?' the accused taunted him, pointing his weapon at him. 'Do you believe I can do the impossible? You can see for yourself where I stand and where you are, you blockhead! You stumbled over your own feet. You can kick others but you haven't learned yet how to walk!'

Tako Kakuta kept a straight face but chuckled inwardly.

Levtan had been brought before the three traders who regarded him with despise. He was relentlessly bombarded with unending questions and was barely able to think of his answers.

'Don't expect mercy from us, you conniving coward!' one of the traders suddenly shouted at him. 'Do you know who I am? I'm Gaxtek's son! I belong to the clan which you have robbed of the fruits of three expeditions to Casters star. Don't you remember me?'

The outcast cringed as if beaten with a whip but a vile look still flickered in his eyes as he yelled back at them: 'You don't have the authority to investigate me! I demand to be heard by the Great Conclave! It's my right! I came to bring information which will save us all from destruction!'

'Bunk!' Gaxtek snarled, clenching his fists.

'I've got proof!' Levtan defied him but a moment later he begged: 'If you treat me and my clan decently . . .'

Gaxtek laughed in his face. 'You're a notorious liar, you scum!'

The tall, slender trader nodded his head in agreement. The second, somewhat stouter man who had only posed an occasional question during the ceaseless cross-examination, commented: 'We'll submit his statement to Goszul. Let the patriarch decide between truth and lie I recommend that he be taken back to his cell.'

Levtan grinned maliciously. He was convinced that he would be vindicated and honored the next day and these three traders would be the first to feel his vengeance. He gave Gaxtek a vicious look before the two guards led him away to be locked up again.

'Did you see his eyes?' Gaxtek was asked when the traders were alone again.

Pensively he looked at his companions, 'Yes,' he replied, 'I saw his look and I got the message. What if Levtan actually speaks the truth for once and produces proof of his claims? I think I'll go and visit Etztak . . .'

'Why do you want to speak to that intemperate old man?' the tall slender trader asked in surprise.

'To plant suspicion against Levtan's testimony. Etztak's the only patriarch who's had the shattering experience of a fight against Perry Rhodan and was forced by him to flee for his life. Topthor the Mounder lost his fleet. Haven't you realized yet what Levtan's role is?'

They had failed to grasp the significance and stared at the questioning man.

'Then I'll tell you the same as I'll tell Etztak: Levtan is a diabolical time bomb planted by Perry Rhodan to make us perish!'

Chapter Six

THE PENULTIMATE MOMENT

Kitai Ishibashi had applied his will in order to be placed alone in a separate cell with his mates and not in the large hall where most of the *LEV's* crew were held.

Only Levtan was thrown into a single cell. The patriarchs of the Springers considered him their most valuable cource of information and attached only secondary importance to his crew.

The mutants were amazed to see that the native Goszuls were used as help in the prison. John Marshall had succeeded twice in starting a conversation with a Goszul through the peephole in the door but each time a guard of the Springers had appeared and broken off their contact.

Nevertheless, John Marshall had been able by virtue of his telepathic gifts to gather some interesting information. After Yokida the Telekin had thoroughly searched their cell for hidden electronic bugs, Marshall whispered to his friends:

'These Goszuls are all brainwashed and enslaved. They're forbidden to return to their families. And do you know why? So that the people of Goszul will be prevented from knowing the old fact that space travel has been achieved elsewhere!'

Tako Kakuta didn't trust his ears. 'How could they not – with all these spaceships coming and going here? The Goszuls aren't blind!'

This was an obvious question for John and he explained: 'I've already noted something about a certain lane of approach when Levtan came in for a landing. Now I understand why they used such special precautions . . .'

'What a charming clan from the tribe of the Arkonides!' Tama Yokida murmured. 'This place gives me the creeps.' He made it plain that he toyed with the idea of lifting the solid prison door out of its hinges with his telekinetic powers.

Rhodan had put Marshall in charge of the task force. He merely looked at Tama Yokida who deeply sighed and said in resignation: 'Oh, shucks!'

Steps were heard along the corridor. Their cell door, which Yokida wanted to move telekinetically, was opened. A guard and two Goszuls peered inside.

'Come out!' the guard ordered. He held a raygun in his hand.

They left the cell but Tako Kakuta dawdled. He and Marshall had just cooked up something.

When the three mutants walked past the Goszuls they looked at them with exceptional curiosity. Kitai Ishibashi detected sympathy and regret in their eyes despite a rather vacant look.

John Marshall probed the confused thoughts of the guard. The man knew only that they were to be taken to an interrogation. The entire fortress was buzzing with one acute topic, namely Levtan.

The tall thin-faced Australian tuned in on the thoughts of the Goszuls. He found what Kitai Ishibashi had also read in their eyes as well as the silent question. *Why did you come to our world? Don't you know you'll never be allowed to leave . . . like us?*

The guard berated Tako Kakuta who was still standing in the cell: 'How long do you think I'm going to wait for you?'

At this moment John Marshall couldn't suppress an amused smile. He had perceived the question in Tako's mind: *Is this ruffian also going to kick me from behind?*

The guard saw Marshall's grin and took it as an offense. He jerked up his black raygun, pointed it at Marshall and threatened him with a dangerous glint in his eye: 'Cut out your grin or . . .'

Kitai Ishibashi stepped in. His will took possession of the guard. John Marshall's face had become rigid when the guard dropped his weapon and said pleasantly to Tako Kakuta: 'Come, my friend! Don't keep us waiting!'

Kitai Ishibashi discontinued his effort. The short treatment sufficed to keep the guard in good humour till they reached the interrogation room. Suddenly he felt the gaze of the two Goszuls directed at him and saw Marshall's gesture. Both Goszuls seemed to have weak telepathic propensities which however had been blocked by hypnosis and almost completely destroyed.

The experience had an unsettling influence on the Japanese. Had Perry Rhodan figured when he designed his plan that they would encounter telepaths on Goszul's planet?

The two serfs followed them a few steps behind. The now very amiable guard opened the door for them and invited them politely to enter.

Etztak gaped flabbergasted at the guard and the four other traders also expressed shock beyond belief.

'Out with you traitors!' Etztak shouted in a cracking voice. 'Get them out of here and put them back in their cell!'

The guard wanted to take them back but Etztak roared: 'You stay here!' and aimed his gun at him. 'Gaxtek and Hor, you take them back!'

Kitai Ishibashi had used the little time he had to sway the patriarch of the Etztak clan and cause Gaxtek and Hor to lead them back to the same cell from which they had been shoved out.

John Marshall sensed the complications. He listened to Etztak's thoughts and was overcome by the most serious misgivings. As soon as they had returned to their cell and the magnetic locks had snapped shut, he warned his friends.

Kitai Ishibashi turned pale and whispered: 'You mean Etztak will put the guard through the brain analyzer?'

Tako Kakuta spoke up: 'John, tell me quickly where the guard is now!'

Marshall concentrated intensely. Nobody in the cell dared breathe loudly.

Could he locate him again? Why did it take so long?

Finally Marshall lifted his face, which was bathed in perspiration. His eyes had lost their shine. 'He's being carried off in the custody of six men in an armored car.'

'Where is he, Marshall?' Tako Kakuta asked, ready to jump off.

The telepath shook his head dejectedly. 'I receive many streams of thought but each one spells death for you if you jump in, Tako. The six men who are taking our guard to the brain analyzer keep their fingers on the trigger. I can feel it, they'll squeeze . . .'

'Where is he?' the frail Japanese repeated his question in a cool, determined tone.

Marshall informed him that one of the henchmen was thinking about the huge dock where the vehicle passed by.

There were only three mutants left in the cell. Tako Kakuta, the teleporter, had leaped to an uncertain fate after the guard who was bound to reveal their secret in the brain analyzer.

Etztak and the other traders had already left the interrogation room before the guard was led away to the brain-analyzer. He took a car and raced to Goszul. Without waiting to be announced he rushed in and broke up a meeting but Etztak cared little about it.

He burst out with the ardor of a young man in the knowledge that Perry Rhodan presented a peril which could hardly be underestimated. He had learned it from bitter experience.

When Etztak saw Goszul grinning superciliously he suddenly regained his calm. Abruptly he broke off his report. 'You don't believe me yet?' he asked coldly.

'No more than I believe in the world of Eternal Life,' Goszul replied. 'Ever since you met Rhodan you can't think straight any more, Etztak. You've never recovered from that shock. I can think straight but I've no objection if you want to use the brainalyzer to find out what the guard knows.'

The trader was utterly callous and completely unmoved by the fact that the guard would be turned into an idiot by the treatment of the brain prober.

Suddenly the door was flung open. Gaxtek was on the threshold, shouting excitedly: 'One of the escorts has killed the guard!'

'This is the work of Rhodan!' Etztak called out, perhaps unknowingly setting the course of future events.

Patriarch Goszul laughed uproariously and slapped his belly.

Tako Kakuta, the slight Japanese teleporter, was back in the cell from which he had silently vanished 15 minutes earlier. He appeared at the same spot where he had left before. His childlike face with the bulging forehead looked small and exhausted. He kept wiping the sweat from his brow and was breathing rapidly.

His friends waited with superhuman patience for his report. Only Marshall knew already what had transpired but he remained silent.

Then Tako Kakuta said in a toneless voice: 'He's dead. They stood around him when I arrived at the vehicle and a raygun went off at the moment I disappeared again.'

He didn't go on to tell them about the half dozen hazardous jumps he had performed while searching for the armored car. He thought this was immaterial. Neither did he relate to them that he had triggered an alarm with his second jump when he landed on the transparent roof of the spaceship dock.

His friends looked at him quietly. They could explain themselves why one of the six henchmen had blasted his raygun. All of them well remembered the shock when the teleporter appeared for the first time like a phantom from nowhere.

In the middle of the night Marshall suddenly woke up. He was startled by strange thought impulses. Silent cries of an anguished soul, so confused that it took him some time to decipher them. Then he finally realized from whence the impulses originated. In the adjacent cell a Goszul who had been condemned to death despaired.

Marshall woke up his friends and talked to them about the impressions he had received.

As far as the mutants had been able to glean Goszul's Planet was a pitiful world of slaves. The traders mercilessly oppressed a peaceful and good-natured people.

'Descendants of the Arkonides?' Kitai Ishibashi explained in astonishment. 'Do these Goszuls also belong to the race of the Arkonides?'

His question was not strange at all. Long before the sinking of Atlantis the Arkonides had come to Earth like Gods and were never seen again. Nonetheless the legend had lived on in the stories of all people. Here on Goszul's Planet fate must have chosen a similar course and this peaceful race of brothers from the same race had been subjected to serfdom.

'These tyrannical Springers!' Tama Yokida gnashed his teeth while he continued listening to Marshall's whispering.

The Goszuls had retrogressed to a more primitive state. Their science and technology were comparable to that on Earth in the 17th century. They believed they saw Gods when patriarch Goszul and his clan landed among them. But the Springers saw only a world to be exploited – the most profitable business of their lives. Goszul took possession of the second planet of the sun 221-Tatlira. The harmless population was forced into slavery by hypno-training and the men were deported to a place where he built his power centrum with the help of the mighty trader organization.

The chattel in the next cell had lost his mind in his agony. His mental breakdown had cracked the hypno-block and each time he experienced a sane moment and recognized the hopelessness of his situation, he remembered what the traders had done to him and his brothers.

The breathlessly listening mutants were distracted by the noise of loud steps. Three guards marched along the corridor, passed their cell and stopped next door.

Kakuta, Ishibashi and Yokida could hear the magnetic locks spring open and the door swing back and then they recoiled in horror.

Marshall saw the guard raising his raygun and aiming at the condemned man. He shared the agony of the slave.

Then there was nothing!

John Marshall had failed to hear anything but Ishibashi, Yokida and Kakuta had picked up the typical sound of the hissing beam.

Patriarch Goszul was not the incompetent fool for which Etztak had gradually come to take him. Goszul had ordered an investigation of the shooting which had occurred when the guard was taken to the brain analyzer. Sharer, a member of his clan, gave him the report.

The patriarch listened silently. He had not forgotten Etztak's exclamation: 'This is the work of Rhodan!' He didn't underestimate this man who lived in a small far away world in a half-deserted branch of the Galaxy, a place called Terra.

Now he asked his first question: 'Who besides the nitwit that killed the guard has seen that shadow?'

'Nobody! I've queried each one intensively. But the man standing next to the one firing the fatal shot claims to have felt a blow on his back.'

Despite his age Goszul was a man with remarkable mental faculties. He always unerringly picked the most important detail out of a set of complicated facts. And so he insisted in this case: 'I want to hear from you, Sharer, the exact words the man told you.'

Sharer briefly reflected. ' "I saw Plugg shoot and at the same moment a fist hit my back. Plugg couldn't have pushed against me because he swayed and shot while he was off balance. Lusud on my left side hadn't yet understood what was happening. He stood completely still." This is the precise text of his statement, Patriarch Goszul.'

'And now Plugg's account, Sharer, also word for word!'

'He said: "I was surprised by an attack. A man had jumped on my back and tried to strangle me with his left hand. I can still feel on my neck where he pressed me with his thumb. The jolt caused me to lose my balance and I stumbled. While staggering I must have triggered the ray-gun and shot the guard. Almost immediately the strangling hand and the man on my back were gone. There was nothing . . . nothing at all . . ."'

'Did Plugg show you where the thumb was pressed against his neck?'

Sharer hastened to demonstrate where Plugg claimed to have been choked by a thumb.

The patriarch mulled over the testimony for a minute and then asked to be connected with the prison. 'The warden!' he demanded.

The guard officer answered at once.

Goszul spoke crisply into the mike: 'Make an inspection of Levtan's crew and take a count to check that each prisoner is present. Post two guards in front of each cell where they're kept. Report to me at once if one or more men are missing!'

He turned back to Sharer, when the loudspeaker clicked and the picture screen started to flicker. It was the spaceport calling. The pinched face of a man became visible. 'Ottek speaking!' said the man. 'We've finished the search of the *LEV XIV*. Nothing of importance was found except a few pieces of equipment which must have been brought in from that planet Earth or Venus . . .'

'And you call that "nothing was found!"' Goszul bellowed. 'Is there nobody left in our clan on whom I can still depend? I want you to take all objects which originated on Earth or Venus to the laboratory for a thorough test! Do you hear me? And where are those documents Levtan is constantly talking about, the proof of his absurd statements about Rhodan's huge installations and spaceships on Venus? Did you find that, Ottek?'

'We were unable to locate any reference to it, Patriarch Goszul,' the ugly man said meekly and cringed.

'Search everything again with rays. I must have proof in my hands when the Great Conclave convenes. Levtan's documents must be on the *LEV XIV*. If you don't find them you can take the next ship to the mines! Don't forget it!' Goszul grinned viciously and turned the telecom off.

'Sharer, I want to be alone! Leave me!'

When Goszul was left alone with his troubles, he cursed Rhodan with so much hate that Etztak would have delightedly slapped his old friend Goszul on the shoulder if he could only have heard him.

The prison door behind which Rhodan's mutants were confined flew open. They were menaced by five rayguns as they sleepily rose and blinked into the light. A man loudly counted to four and another one behind him said: 'That's right! That completes it.'

The door was banged shut again and the magnetic locks were secured. Two guards remained at the door and the others went on.

Rhodan's taskforce exchanged glances. They had easily guessed the reason for the control check. It was the reaction to the death of the guard on his way to the brain analyzer.

'The traders' suspicion has been aroused,' Marshall whispered. 'One more incident they don't know how to explain is all it'll take to get wise to the idea that there must be mutants among the *LEV's* crew.'

Etztak sought out the company of the patriarch Gaxtek, the trader who had been cheated many years ago of the reward of his labor by Levtan. Gaxtek's son was Etztak's most ardent supporter. He had not forgotten the murderous look in Levtan's eyes and was constantly reminded that the Gaxtek clan would be just as rich as Etztak's if they had not been victimized by a ruthless member of their own people.

Etztak countered all remonstrations. 'Perry Rhodan is strong but he has weaknesses. I can't be dissuaded that he would have attacked us long ago if he weren't deterred by some crucial drawback. Somewhere he's weak . . . but weak men can also be dangerous. They try to compensate for their weakness with cunning. And Levtan serves Rhodan's stratagem. Could you think of a better opportunity to eliminate all Galactic traders with one stroke than the Great Conclave? Tell me, Gaxtek, what would you do in Rhodan's place?'

In his overwhelming hatred for Perry Rhodan, Etztak underestimated the patriarch Goszul. Goszul had already pondered and answered the same question. He took appropriate measures. More than 50 messengers were dispatched to the patriarchs of the clans and the spaceport had been put on alert.

Not one of the patriarchs slept the night before the Great Conclave. The destroyer formations of the traders and their few battleships raced with whining engines along the take-off lanes into the clear night sky.

But Goszul was not alone concerned with an attack from outer space. He also considered the possibility of sabotage in the Great Conclave. Like Etztak he had tried to put himself in Rhodan's place and had come to the same conclusion that Rhodan's armor must have a serious chink.

However Goszul didn't wrack his brain trying to find the weakness. He marked the spot with an X and figured in his calculations that this unknown X represented a critical danger for him.

The agitation in his waiting room kept growing irresistibly. He could hear Sharer talking excitedly. The telecom next to his armchair buzzed and the commander of the heavy rocket installations reported that all positions were manned and ready to fire.

Goszul listened silently to his report and when his picture faded away he snarled a name: Perry Rhodan.

He could not remember that there had ever been a time in the history of the Galactic traders when the acts of an enemy had necessitated a convocation of the Great Conclave.

Sharer entered. 'All clans have been notified. Each patriarch and each observer to the Great Conclave will be identified by name through members of two other clans before admittance to the assembly hall.'

Goszul was struck by an idea. 'I want to set the opening

of the Great Conclave two hours earlier! Sharer, arrange for the messengers to advise the patriarchs of the change only at the last minute!'

After Sharer had left he couldn't get rid of a nagging feeling and wished that the Great Conclave were already over. Once more he cursed Perry Rhodan's name.

Chapter Seven

DRAMA ON GOSZUL

'Contact!'

The word was repeated four times – on the *Stardust II* and the three cruisers. They had waited in vain for hours for a pre-arranged signal from the task force but it failed to come through.

Rhodan's fleet was standing by more than 10 million miles away – four tiny craft in infinite space with extremely delicate hyper-sensors which had just registered the start of a great number of spaceships on Goszul's Planet.

'It looks pretty bad,' Bell said softly so that only Perry Rhodan could hear.

They were joined by the Arkonide scientist Khrest. 'At the risk of repeating myself,' he began, 'it's getting very hard for me to believe that our mutants were successful. The alarm on the planet speaks for itself.'

Perry Rhodan slowly rose from the pilot seat. As he stood before the Arkonide, who was a head taller than he, there was nevertheless an amazing resemblance for two people of different races.

'I've faith in the ability of my men,' Rhodan replied quietly. 'And I assume that the positronic brain gives them a good chance. Would you like to take a look at the prognosis with me, Khrest?'

Meanwhile the rangefinder continually supplied new data. The battlefleet of the traders circled the planet from which it had started in ever increasing trajectories. They searched systematically through space, a worrisome fact which was pointed out by Khrest on their way to the positron.

'I know!' Rhodan answered.

'They'll soon obtain our bearings the same way we've observed their take-off,' Khrest warned with great urgency.

'We've already retreated after the traders' fleet was launched.' Perry's answer contained a gentle rebuke. 'I don't want to endanger the four men unnecessarily.'

Khrest stared at him with astonishment. Once again he couldn't help admiring the near perfection of this Earthling. He didn't disregard the fact that Rhodan had acquired the wealth of Arkonide knowledge through him but neither was he inclined to overestimate it. In the final analysis it solely depended on the person whether he could apply his knowledge or not. Perry Rhodan made such skilful use of these revelations that the Arkonide was proud of him.

Ron stated the chances for success of the mutant team in cold figures.

'This is really . . .'

'. . . very good, isn't it?' Perry interrupted. 'The brain machine on Venus has computed the chances to be 0.4 and . . .'

Khrest flared up, fire in his eyes: 'And with a probability for success of only 0.4% you have risked the lives of four men?'

Words failed Khrest when Rhodan nodded.

'Yes!' said Perry Rhodan and the firm 'Yes' taught Khrest an astonishing truth that was further driven home by the remainder of Rhodan's answer: 'Success chances 0.4% plus Man! Khrest, we're not like the Arkonides who are content to spend their waking hours with their eyes fixed on a dream machine. That's the simple reason why the chances of our mutant team are so considerably greater. "Plus Man" is an ingredient which cannot be evaluated by the big positronic brain on Venus . . . because it was built by Arkonides!'

The stern voice of the rangefinder officer broke in: 'Three destroyers veered away from the Springers' formation and seem to be headed toward us . . .'

'Increase acceleration by five!' Rhodan quickly called to Bell.

'Did the Springers find our position?'

The unanswered question hung heavy in the command center.

'I'll go and take a look outside,' Tako Kakuta had said a few minutes earlier. 'I must know what's going on. Something seems to have gone awry. I'll be back in 15 minutes.'

Nobody objected and the teleporter disappeared. He landed in a daring leap on the spaceport. The place was lavishly lit up brighter than day. Tako Kakuta closed his eyes in the blinding light and leaped to the outer limits of the spaceport. Once he was outside the flood of light he took time to survey the landing field.

By accident he had landed in the vicinity of the *LEV XIV*. He edged a little closer and saw traders come and go through the big hatch of the ship. This activity aroused his curiosity. The next moment the place where Tako Kakuta had just stood was empty and he materialized inside the *LEV XIV* in a little room which was frequented only for a private purpose. The door to the toilet stood open and two traders were talking outside. Kakuta was pleased to hear that they complained about the patriarch Goszul using the most derogatory language and that Levtan was accorded no less abusive terms. He learned with amusement that they were still trying to find some kind of written proof of Levtan's contentions.

He had heard enough and began to concentrate his thoughts on the large building at the edge of the spaceport which he had seen when the Springers transported him to the prison. And then he jumped.

He appeared again in the shadow of the large building. There was no need for him to hide. He didn't differ from the Springers in appearance and clothing. Leisurely he walked around a corner and approached a group of men who were standing and talking at the entrance.

Tako Kakuta saw too late that a guard was among the group. The guard had already noticed him and seemed to be suspicious when he walked into the light out of the shadows. With a forceful movement of his left arm the guard cleared his line of fire and aimed his gun at Kakuta.

The little Japanese in the guise of a Springer kept his cool.

'Come here' he growled but instead of waiting for him to come, the guard went forward. 'Who are you? And why did you loiter near the bombs?'

All Kakuta could hear was 'bombs'. Instantaneously he absorbed everything around him: the location of the building in relation to the spaceport, the brightly lit façade, the factory hall opposing it, the wide street and the house to the right where apparently the bombs were stored.

'Can't you talk?' the guard roared.

The cluster of men who had carried on a lively conversation now became curious. Two of them approached slowly.

Tako Kakuta weighed the danger of the situation. It obviously was nearing a most awkward dilemma and he didn't dare perform his teleportation. To show his trick would have meant to give away Rhodan's plan and to ruin their mission.

'My name is Brom and I belong to the Gaxtek clan,' he stated briskly and hoped secretly that nobody from Gaxtek's clan was present.

When the guard grinned broadly, showing his rotten teeth, Tako sensed trouble but he was far from realizing the full extent of the impending catastrophe.

'Then you must be from the near ship *GAX XXII,*' the guard queried him warily. 'I know all the others but I've never seen you.'

'*GAX XXII*!' a loud voice came from the background. 'That's my ship. What's the matter?'

'Stop shouting and come here!' the guard called to him, turning halfway around. 'This man claims to be from your ship. Do you know him? Take a look at him . . .' He had turned his head back again, not wanting to let the suspect out of his eyes for too long and the words stuck in his throat when he failed to see his quarry.

Tako Kakuta couldn't think of another way out except teleporting. The trader from the *GAX XXII* who had spoken up had presented him with a desperate opportunity of which he took quick advantage. As the entire audience paid attention to the Springer, Kakuta performed a little jump to the corner of the building.

He swiftly considered all possibilities in utmost coolness. The Springers couldn't be allowed to recognise that he was a mutant and should be convinced that his disappearance was nothing else but a normal flight.

Tako's heart was beating fast. One of the onlookers had seen him turn around the corner, which greatly helped to improve the situation for him.

Now he dashed away. He kept in mind that the gun brandished by the guard was not a lethal weapon but a paralyzing gun with a limited range, giving him a chance for his flight. He ran like a regular fugitive under the cover of darkness but he came closer to the store of bombs and where bombs are kept there are guards.

It's the same everywhere, he thought, as he heard them shouting in the dark: 'Halt!' The Springers were close on his heels and one of them screamed at the guards: 'Don't let him get away!'

Kakuta jumped and teleported himself in midair, descending breathlessly next to a revetment of heavy rockets.

Two soldiers were discussing something and the mutant listened to each word. They talked about the alarm and wondered why Goszul had sent messengers to the patriarchs instead of using regular channels of radio communication to broadcast his instructions.

'Did you notice something?' Tako heard one of the soldiers ask, feeling uneasy when he came closer.

Rather than wait to be bumped into by him, Tako disappeared and materialized again in the cell. His first question was: 'Did I stay away longer than 15 minutes?'

Patriarch Goszul arose with pride when the entrance of the last participant in the Great Conclave was announced.

Till a few minutes before he had been under a cloud of ominous misgivings. Now he felt relieved of these crushing forebodings and sunned himself in the respect rendered to him by all his peers as the discoverer and conqueror of this planet. He had been unanimously elected to preside over the Great Conclave.

Goszul opened the conference of the Galactic traders with a short speech. He greeted all the attending notables personally without mentioning a single name. While he spoke the introductory words his sharp eyes searched for one particular patriarch among the more than 1200: Etztak.

He was unable to find him even after he sat down again and neither could he discover Etztak's sons. He wanted to give instructions to an aide to find out in which row Etztak had taken his seat when the name of Perry Rhodan was mentioned for the first time by a speaker and Goszul instantly forgot all about his friend.

'. . . the sovereignty of the Galactic traders has been threatened in our sphere of influence. Topthor the Mounder has paid with his ship and his life for Etztak's call for help. Perry Rhodan, the inhabitant of a planet called Earth by the human race, has wielded the powerful armaments of the Arkonides to defy us. Arkon's Imperium is in a state of stagnation. We're the rightful heirs. Nothing prevents us from asking the Mounders to join us in a common effort to eliminate the planet Earth from the Galaxy by total annihilation. We're a hundred times stronger than Rhodan but we have come to an understanding about our goal. However before we start our discussion we have to grant a hearing to the traitor Levtan.

'We ourselves have created the laws of our clans. In accordance we mete out punishment but we also adhere to them in making amends. Though we must never forget, my Patriarchs, when listening to the testimony of Levtan that he has been in the world of Perry Rhodan. Levtan's statements and alleged proof will have to be thoroughly scrutinized. Examine him with great care before you forgive him, following the code of our clans and removing the stigma of the pariah from him.

'Examine him prudently, even if you believe he's lying!

'Examine him as if your life depends on this investigation!

'Examine him because it *is* a matter of life or death for us! Perry Rhodan means *death!*'

Stunned silence followed the speech. The exhortation had been performed with suggestive force.

The silence still prevailed when Levtan was brought in, escorted by six robots, and led down the wide center aisle. He was placed in a chair from where he could see the presidium on the dais as well as all participants in the Great Conclave.

Levtan held his gaze, which reflected naked fear, fixed on Goszul. The patriarch rose up again and looked at him sternly, his arms folded over his chest, before he addressed his first question to him: 'Pariah Levtan, where are the documents to prove your claims about Perry Rhodan?'

There was an echo reverberating in the hall.

Rhodan! it called back hauntingly.

Goszul saw several patriarchs shudder and turn around to the main entrance. He himself was hardly able to suppress, with great effort, a terrifying shock.

'I've got the proof on my ship,' Levtan replied in a whisper.

'Where?' Goszul asked sharply, adding with his next breath: 'Don't expect to prolong your life by such tactics!'

With a gesture of utmost despair Levtan pleaded vehemently: 'Didn't I return voluntarily?' he cried out, the slits of his eyes narrowing. 'Didn't I return for the sole purpose of showing you the way to destroy Perry Rhodan? Who among you knows Rhodan?'

And the echo jeered: *Rhodan!*

Again Goszul noticed that some of the patriarchs were startled and whirled around to look at the entrance as if they expected to see Perry Rhodan.

Goszul thought quickly. The echo which had already come back twice to haunt them had to be reduced to a minimum by a careful formulation of his words.

'Where are the documents?' Goszul asked the pariah in an imperative tone.

'In the command center of my ship. In the guidance system compartment,' Levtan answered submissively.

Goszul's old eyes flashed like those of a youthful hunter to the members of his clan standing at the main entrance and he called to them in a loud commanding voice: 'Get it out of there! I want to have it here at once!' And then he said to Levtan in a calmer tone: 'Tell us about Rhodan!'

He couldn't take the word back. The echo brought it back: *Rhodan!*

Goszul felt the first drops of sweat on his furrowed brow. 'Start talking!' Goszul bellowed uncontrollably at Levtan. He was slowly losing his composure under the influence of the many patriarchs who succumbed to the sinister echo and sat whispering low, putting their heads together.

Finally Levtan began his report.

The situation for Perry Rhodan and his fleet had eased up. The Springer ships still kept circling around Goszul's Planet but they didn't patrol beyond a distance of three million miles from it. More important was the fact that measurements on the *Stardust II* had determined that the traders exclusively used structure sensors which worked on the principle of hyper-gravitation. It barely permitted them to make a rough measurement within the range of one astronomical unit but it became extremely effective beyond the 90-million-mile limit.

Perry Rhodan's ships were standing 20 million miles away from Goszel's Planet waiting for a message or an attack. They waited for something to evolve but nothing happened.

There was a noise in the receiver. The built-in descrambler decoded the radio call which, to the human ear, was only audible as a short beep.

Rhodan read the text and hid his disappointment. The message came from Terrania. It had been sent by Col. Freyt to the administrator Perry Rhodan. He handed it silently to Bell who suspected what it contained. Disgustedly he asked: 'Paper war from down there?'

Down there – was the Earth, finally united under Perry Rhodan without power blocs outshouting each other that they were the strongest. There still remained three interest groups on good old Earth but their main task was reduced to accomplishing the withering away of their separate states.

'Read it!' Perry urged his friend.

Bell read reluctantly. 'There are still a few ambitious men left who are trying to make politics. Well, Freyt will rap their knuckles. Shall I answer it, Perry?'

'No!' Rhodan said tersely; pulled the note from Bell's fingers and handed it to Julian Tifflor, who stood next to him. 'Throw it into the shredder, Tifflor!'

Without looking Julian Tifflor threw the note into a grill. The paper simply dissolved without a trace.

Rhodan quickly glanced at the young man. His soft face, where tough missions under difficult conditions already had left their mark, was deceiving like his dreamy brown eyes. Julian Tifflor was anything but soft and pliable. He was the most dependable and successful astronaut of the young generation that had dedicated its life to Perry Rhodan.

'You seem to yearn to be with John Marshall, Tifflor?'

There was a fire in Tifflor's brown eyes. The spark had shown the stuff Julian Tifflor was made of. For a fraction of a second he had revealed his thoughts but his voice sounded calm when he answered his chief: 'Sir, one can't always be in the front lines!'

The nerve-wracking waiting in the command center of the *Stardust II* was interrupted by a sudden call from the observation officer: 'Strong sudden radioactive disturbance on Goszul's Planet! Locally limited . . . Evaluation follows in a moment!'

Rhodan had to wait in spite of his impatience. He began to guess something. In apprehension he looked at his watch and then asked curtly: 'Please give me the local time of the second planet!'

'45:71,' someone at the chronometer panel answered. This was about noon Terra time. The day on Goszul's Planet had about reached the zenith and there was still no message from the team of mutants, contrary to what had been arranged with them.

'Evaluation!' the rangefinder officer reported again. 'Radiation inside the capital city! Locally limited to diameter of 300 to 500 feet!'

Marshall, Yokida, Ishibashi and Kakuta were uppermost in the thoughts of all those in the command center. The mutants had failed to give a sign of life on the agreed channel.

Chapter Eight

THE CEREBRAL INQUISITOR

John Marshall picked up the time telepathically. Locally it was 23:104. The four men in the prison cell converted it to Terrestrial time. It was about 9 in the morning on Earth.

'The food and board in this establishment leaves something to be desired,' the telekinetic Tama Yokida stated. 'I suggest that we scrounge up some chow ourselves.' He ogled the massive cell door and toyed again with the idea of lifting it off its hinges with his t.k. powers.

'No, no!' said Marshall who had intercepted his thoughts again. 'It won't be necessary. They're coming to pick us up to attend the Great Conclave!'

His friends looked at him suspiciously. There was something in his voice that didn't sound right.

'Yes,' the telepath added to his announcement, 'but not as guests, as witnesses for Levtan. The wretched fellow must have acted like a madman and insisted on his demand that his clan be heard too.'

'A fine chief of clan he is!' the usually reserved Tako Kakuta said. 'My father would have behaved differently! When will they come to get us, Marshall?'

'The guards are already on the way. They all talk about

Levtan. They now know where he kept the documents hidden. Goszul is said to have rushed some men from his clan to the *LEV XIV* to dig them out of the guidance system compartment . . .'

Kitai Ishibashi interrupted Marshall. 'I got interested in that myself one time. I would never have suspected they could be hidden there. For heaven's sake, did they discover our cache of arms?'

'The guards aren't thinking about that,' Marshall replied and listened. 'Don't you hear them coming?'

Steps were audible in the corridor. The firm stamping of the robots was unmistakable.

The prison door was pushed open. Three paralysis guns and two impulse beamers were pointed at them.

'Get out!' one of the Springers barked. Judging from his uniform he was an officer.

Rhodan's task force silently left the inhospitable dungeon. They were transported to the Great Conclave in a large armored vehicle. Tako Kakuta believed that he had been in such a vehicle yesterday when the unlucky guard was taken to the brain analyzer.

When they arrived and climbed out they were surrounded by a platoon of fighter robots.

'If these toy soldiers accompany us into the hall and keep us in their rays they can make life rough for us,' Tama Yokida thought and tried a test to find out how heavy one of the robots was. He selected the metallic automaton who stood farthest behind and could not be observed by his soulless mates nor by the Springers.

Tama Yokida only 'played' a little with him. His effort

to lift the robot two feet off the ground was no greater than bending his little finger. The experiment had taken less than a second and Tama Yokida was satisfied with the result.

He followed his friends calmly into the vast assembly hall. Yet he held his breath when he saw more than 1000 patriarchs seated in rows. There were more chiefs of clans than he had expected to see and he was awed by the presence of such a spectacular crowd.

Marshall soon discovered the fact that there was not a single patriarch in the hall who believed one word Levtan had told them about Perry Rhodan. They gave no credence to the alleged proof of the pariah.

The little group was completely surrounded by robots and followed by heavily armed Springers. They were led down the wide center aisle of the arched hall to the chairman of the Great Conclave.

Levtan was at his stand, sweating profusely and looking toward his clan like a drowning man. He was at the end of his rope. Nobody trusted his proof – the documents, the reports, the three-dimensional photos and movies.

'Cheap phony tricks!' a patriarch heckled soon after the film had started to run showing the take-off of 22 battleships all bearing the name of *Stardust* and numbered consecutively.

Levtan had shouted back. He knew that his film was no forgery. He had taken these pictures himself on Venus at the risk of his life and had almost fallen into the hands of Rhodan's counter-espionage service. He remembered each detail but here he encountered only the most stupid and agonizing disbelief despite his best intentions of bringing help to the Springers. He was the only one who could show them the way to escape from the perilous plight engendered by Perry Rhodan.

Perry Rhodan – the most formidable power that had ever appeared among the stars and whose strength exceeded many times the Arkonide Imperium at its height!

His voice cracked as he pleaded with them: '. . . and every five days they complete a heavy cruiser. Perry Rhodan seems to make his spaceships spring from the ground on Venus. I've seen it with my own eyes, brothers! Remember that I'm one of you! I've been treated like a dog by Perry Rhodan. He hates us and will destroy all of us if we attack him. He'll hunt down our clans one by one . . .'

Levtan was jolted by a ray which caused him to break off in the middle of his sentence and the film continued to the end without being interrupted by his diatribe.

Etztak, the patriarch of the Orlgans clan, watched the crew of the *LEV XIV* being marched in. Couched deeply in his armchair and half hidden behind the hulking patriarch Slurd, he had observed the proceedings with complete concentration, remaining unimpressed by the developments. The film had not caused him to change his mind either. He was suspicious of the pictures and doubted the existence of 22 battleships, not to mention Levtan's ridiculous claim that Perry Rhodan constructed a heavy cruiser on Venus every five days. Etztak could not be shaken in his opinion that even in this day and age it took considerable time to create such miracles.

'I would like to know why Goszul has dragged these

fellows out of the prison,' Etztak said to Virn, the patriarch of the Sanko clan who sat to the right of him stroking his beard in constant excitement. 'Are we supposed to listen to a repetition of these despicable lies?'

On Etztak's left sat Gaxtek who almost had been ruined by Levtan's fraudulent manipulations many years ago. He nudged the patriarch of the Orlgans clan and drew his attention to the activity going on among the committee of nine patriarchs on the dais.

One of Levtan's documents was passed from hand to hand by the members of the committee while Levtan's crew and clan slowly closed in around the suspect captain.

Three robots were posted in the background ready to unleash their deadly rayguns and kill the outcast men. Their positronic aim was concentrated only on the outcasts.

Etztak craned his neck to look over the broad shoulders of Slurd at the men on the dais. He narrowed his eyes and thought he was suffering from hallucinations. He saw the committee examine one of Levtan's papers with inexplicable seriousness and the patriarch Goszul was right in the middle of the eagerly debating group. Now Goszul raised his eyes and directed a question at Levtan.

Etztak didn't trust his ears. He was astonished by the tone in which Goszul asked his question.

The pariah saw his chances improve. Until now he had either shrieked his answers or begged and cried. Suddenly Levtan began to blare out his assertions: 'Daily output of destroyers class C, three units, class G, four units and eight units of the biggest class H.'

Once more Goszul urgently consulted with the presiding

committee of the great Conclave and then decided: 'Please show the second film!'

Etztak fell back in his armchair, disappearing again behind the broad back of the giant patriarch Slurd. He paid no attention to the projected film and didn't respond to Gaxtek's questions. He was only physically in the meeting hall. Mentally he was on board his ship and his ship was in a fight with Perry Rhodan's cruisers. Something had happened there. An impossibility had become reality. Etztak delved deeper into the problem, trying to solve what had occurred.

He was oblivious to his environment, the only patriarch who failed to take part in the Great Conclave.

Rhodan's team mingled with Levtan's clan. They had moved closer together, almost in the center of the shipmates, and watched the film together with the patriarchs. They would have been enthusiastic about the film – if it had depicted the truth. The three-dimensional movie showed a tremendous battle in space between Perry Rhodan's battleships and destroyer squadrons with a numerically far superior opponent. It all looked highly impressive.

Levtan had found his voice again and commented: 'Location of battle: Xader's Cloud!'

Xader's Cloud was a notation taken from the star catalog of the Galactic traders. Rhodan had carefully taken into consideration the evidence Levtan had to provide to make the film seem credible.

The Springer catalog had served him in good stead. Xader's Cloud was situated at the opposite end of the

Milky Way and had the reputation among the traders of being the deadliest region of the Galaxy. So far, any ship which approached Xader's Cloud within less than five astronomical units was destined to be lost without a trace. Not even a call for help had ever been heard nor had a single auxiliary ship returned to relate the story of the disasters which had befallen them – and here Perry Rhodan tore the veil from the secret of Xader's Cloud.

The spaceships of the race inhabiting the Cloud looked ominously strange. They consisted of three huge spheres welded together. The sphere in the middle appeared to have a diameter of more than 1500 feet as judged by comparison with Rhodan's battleships.

The film showed Rhodan's awesome victory over the race residing in Xader's Cloud.

When the film ended a terror had been struck in the hearts of the viewers. A hush had fallen over the Great Conclave. Everyone was silent and Levtan was no exception.

Nobody paid attention to the four men of the Levtan clan who huddled close together in the crew. Two of them were hard at work: Kitai Ishibashi, the suggestor, and John Marshall, the telepath. They emanated their powers after the film had furnished the psychological preparation.

With a great effort the Japanese physician and psychologist forced his will on the patriarch Goszul. Ishibashi concentrated his special powers at first on Goszul alone who unknowingly submitted to the uncanny influence of the Strata Method.

Accept the film as truth and believe the evidence you

have seen in the documents! Trust the testimony of Levtan and his clan! Perry Rhodan's power is overwhelming. Desist from your useless attempt to invade the Earth or to attack the base on Venus. You'll fly to your death!

John Marshall had directed his attention to the brains of the committee members presiding over the meeting with Goszul. His powers were not the same as those of Ishibashi but he made it easier for the Japanese to put them in a state of deep hypnosis so that they were convinced they acted of their own volition and merely followed their own reasoning.

The silence in the huge assembly hall was broken by a strident question from the patriarch Resd who demanded an answer from Levtan.

Levtan believed in his own pronouncements. He was convinced he had seen and experienced everything first hand. Moreover, he believed in his professed hatred of Rhodan and it was this vehemently expressed abhorrence which suddenly lent more credence to his harangues.

More and more minds came under the thrall of Ishibashi. Many of the patriarchs realized they would seal their own fate if they assaulted Rhodan.

A panic was growing on the right side of the auditorium and turmoil was about to break out. Levtan shouted his answer in a shrill voice: 'I've witnessed the effect of Rhodan's latest weapon! When he deployed it a mountain chain vanished without leaving a cloud of gas. As I fled they were busy installing these weapons on all ships.'

Goszul spoke up. He sternly demanded silence but the panic was spreading like an insidious poison to all corners.

'Haven't we heard enough? Wasn't the last film from Rhodan's archives sufficient proof? What more evidence do you require than the records already presented to you? Patriarchs of the Galactic traders! A pariah is warning us from venturing on a road to disaster! But far be it from me to persuade anyone. I want you to be convinced in your own mind. It's not feasible to submit the pertinent papers to all you patriarchs but I request instead the audience sitting in the first three rows to step up and inspect the records.'

Kitai Ishibashi accomplished wonders. He had created the panic with his inherent faculties. Growing numbers of brains were caught in his spell. Ever increasing numbers of patriarchs were led to believe that Levtan spoke the truth and they were intimidated by Rhodan's dreadful power.

Tama Yokida and the teleporter Tako Kakuta stood wedged in the middle of the passive pariah clan. They merely observed the events as they unfolded and saw how Rhodan's 'Galactic Interception' mission began to take its toll.

Suddenly Kakuta's heart beat rapidly. Where was Levtan? He had lost sight of him. His view of Levtan's stand was intermittently obstructed by the curious patriarchs who walked up to the dias so that he was able to catch only an occasional glimpse.

Had Goszul called Levtan up to him to elucidate the exhibits with additional explanations? However, Tako Kakuta could not see him there either.

Tama Yokida noticed that his friend had become

restless. 'What's the matter?' he whispered in his ear.

'Levtan is gone,' the teleporter replied in a barely audible voice.

Tama Yokida turned around and saw the robot guards standing at the same place as before holding their ray-guns ready to shoot. 'He must be here.'

'I'll be damned if I can see him! Where is he?' Kakuta murmured as he was gripped and shaken in a storm of anxiety.

He nudged John Marshall. It was almost painful for the Australian to return to the normal world. The disturbance had sapped so much of his strength that he was temporarily incapable of understanding Tako Kakuta's thoughts. The teleporter had to whisper the troublesome news to him.

Marshall, who towered a head above the Japanese teleporter, looked all over for Levtan but it was also in vain. He was nowhere to be seen, neither on the platform where the patriarchs crowded around the committee nor in the wide center aisle.

'Since when do you miss him?' Marshall asked calmly.

'Perhaps 8 or 10 minutes. I don't know exactly. Keep looking for him, Marshall! Now I'm really afraid that something has gone awry!'

Tako Kakuta's excitement was contagious. John Marshall nodded to him and tried to locate Levtan with his telepathic powers.

Etztak saw the patriarchs seated in the first three rows

arise and eagerly rush to the platform to view Levtan's exhibits.

The patriarch of the Orlgans clan jumped up with a speed that belied his age. His chair was close to the center aisle. Mumbling apologies he squeezed past four other elders, stopped in the aisle and looked to the main entrance. He gave a nod and waited for what was to follow.

It took a full minute before Levtan disappeared from his stand. Then a trader coming down from the dais walked by so closely that he brushed against him. The trader apologized and Etztak twisted his face in a grimace.

A couple of minutes later he turned around and slowly ambled away as if he were going out to get a breath of fresh air.

When John Marshall grabbed him painfully by the arm Tako Kakuta knew that something terrible had happened.

'Levtan has been kidnapped by Etztak and the Orlgans clan! They're taking him to the brainalyzer!' Marshall whispered agitatedly.

That will be the end of us, Kakuta thought in a welter of despair. He turned his head to Marshall and stopped in the middle of his movement. Marshall moved his lips. He whispered a hardly audible order to Kitai Ishibashi.

The Suggestor understood that Marshall was able to track down Levtan and to read his thoughts but that he was powerless against the mind machine. Even Kitai was unable to cope with it though fortunately there were other measures he could take.

Marshall received Levtan's feeling of mortal terror. He

communicated all of his thoughts: the desperate struggle of the outcast, the kicking and thrashing around to save himself from the cerebral inquisitor. He knew the fate awaiting him from the many who had been subjected to this torture before him. They all had inevitably paid with the loss of their mind from this ghastly procedure.

Then Marshall concentrated on Etztak's thought-waves. They conveyed a state of extreme alarm. Etztak had become frightfully suspicious and taken immediate action.

John Marshall's mind dwelled briefly on the enslaved people living on this planet and he envisioned the fate threatening the virtually defenseless Earth when the Springers embarked on their invasion. Terra would be doomed to slavery!

Suddenly he monitored a severe jolt. The brain analyzing machine had been turned. It meant the exposure of Perry Rhodan's carefully guarded secret mission of the Galactic Interception.

With the agonizing thought of the impending catastrophe on Terra, John Marshall gave Ishibashi the exact location of the brainalyzer.

Chapter Nine

SHIPWRECKED ON GOSZUL

Etztak watched with a stony face as four men from his clan finally subdued Levtan. The traitor had put up a furious struggle in his defense.

One of Orlgans' sons lay moaning and writhing in a corner, holding his belly with both hands. His youngest nephew kept wiping the blood from his chin. But finally the superior numbers of his opponents overwhelmed Levtan and Etztak looked mercilessly as the clamps were snapped shut on him the machine activated, paralyzing him effectively.

'Out of my way!' Etztak ordered his nephew harshly.

'Yes, sir!' the young trader panted, quickly jumping aside.

Etztak switched on the brain analyzer. Levtan's wild protestations ended. The miserable man surrendered to his terrible fate. He didn't believe in miracles and indeed no miracle occurred to save him.

He threw back his head – the only part of his body he was still able to move – and then he was seized by the irresistible surge of the machine which pervaded the very convolutions of his brain where his thoughts and memories were stored.

'Etztak,' he groaned in final agony, 'the Gods will punish you and your clan for . . .'

He never finished his sentence. Levtan had lost control of his senses. Now he was forced to reveal all his knowledge and bare every secret at the price of losing his mind.

The ruthless patriarch rushed to Levtan's side, 'Make room! ' he demanded and bent over Levtan, examining him anxiously. 'What's the matter with this traitor?' he shouted. 'Is he dying?'

Levtan's head hung down lifelessly.

When Marshall no longer received Levtan's thought impulses he realized that his brain analysis had commenced. A catastrophe was building up with unrelenting speed. Etztak was on the threshold of cracking Levtan's and Perry Rhodan's secret.

More than 1000 light-years away from the Solar System a disaster for Earth was brewing on Goszul's Planet.

John Marshall acted like a cool tactician although the demand almost exceeded his strength. He interceded with circumspection and determination without forgetting any important particulars and even found time to change Kitai Ishibashi's assignment and to give the teleporter Tako Kakuta an appalling order: 'Be ready for a jump to the bomb stockpile! '

The slight Japanese didn't bat an eyelash when he received Marshall's command. He was ready to go in the terrible knowledge that Terra's existence was in jeopardy.

Kitai Ishibashi, the Suggestor, focused once more on Goszul in a joint effort with Marshall.

The bald-headed Springer briefly looked at the *LEV* crew. Without noticing the absence of the outcast captain he saw the three robot guards standing there. He whispered something to the man next to him who promptly rose and soon was seen by Tako Kakuta behind the robots.

The robots were dismissed but the real crew of the *LEV* paid no attention whatsoever. The flurry of excitement over the disappearance of their outlawed commander had already died down in the meantime.

Kitai Ishibashi worked fast but the danger had not yet been stemmed: it remained as great as ever.

Kitai fought, under John Marshall's guidance, a titanic struggle against Levtan's heart. He had to force the heart to stand still – at once!

Etztak was not allowed any indication that would incur his suspicion. Kitai lost all sense of time. He was unaware that the teleporter was standing by for a jump and that Goszul had given instructions for the removal of the three robots, nor did he know that the crew of the *LEV* had been relieved of its anxiety about their vanished commander.

Kitai Ishibashi outdid himself. He held in his hands the fate of an entire world – the Earth!

And there was another spur that gave him formidable strength: Perry Rhodan trusted in his ability and fighting for Perry Rhodan's New Power and the future space empire carried him through the most crucial battle of his life.

Suddenly Levtan's heart muscles were convulsed in a spasm under the hypnotic powers of Ishibashi and Kitai knew that the mentality of the pariah captain no longer functioned in the room where Etztak held sway over Levtan.

Levtan had been prevented from betraying Rhodan's plans. His heart stood still.

But the danger kept swirling closer around the task force in the person of Etztak, the most determined patriarch and protagonist of the Galactic traders who was perfectly willing to use the most reprehensible means to further his goals. 'Take him away!' he bellowed pointing to the dead Levtan. 'Bring in two or three of the other pariahs from his clan. I must know what there's behind these tales about Rhodan!'

Tama Yokida disciplined himself to act as an observer. Rhodan's training had given him the ability to hide his emotions and the usually placid Japanese gave no sign of the turmoil raging inside him.

He saw that Kitai Ishibashi, the Suggestor, gradually consumed his inner strength and detected the first sign of weakening in John Marshall while Tako Kakuta stood beside him concentrating and waiting for his expected teleporting jump. Tama Yokida kept a watch on the patriarchs succumbing to fear in droves as the realization was planted in their brains that it would be utter folly to challenge Perry Rhodan and his planet.

There were no overt signs of the tragic turbulence about to break loose but Tama Yokida sensed the forebodings nevertheless.

'Get a bomb!' Marshall whispered to Kakuta. 'Set it

off in three minutes and blow this place to kingdom come!'

Tako Kakuta didn't jump immediately. He left his spot and squeezed through between Marshall and Ishibashi who closed up together behind him. Now the teleporter jumped off to the arsenal of bombs.

He materialized again in a storage room on top of a stack of bombs. His arrival had not been entirely noiseless. Three of the foot-long bomb casings had given off a metallic sound as they were knocked together. Stockstill he stood, slightly hunched on the bombs, and he didn't have to wait long before hearing approaching steps. They were apparently the steps of a man of blood and flesh. He wondered whether the Springers had used the native inhabitants of the planet to guard the storehouse.

The stack of bombs on which he had landed was about 10 feet high. There were rows of similar piles forming high narrow aisles between them.

The guard turned around the corner. It was a Springer advancing cautiously with an impulse beamer in each hand. He neglected to look up, not suspecting that a danger lurked above.

Tako Kakuta quietly picked up a bomb. It was not very heavy, weighing perhaps 60 pounds, but it had enough weight to suit his purpose.

The armed Springer slowed down his steps and now stood hesitantly exactly below Kakuta.

Dammit, Tako thought with displeasure, this fellow must have the keenest hearing. He seems to know exactly that the noise came from this spot.

Tako took careful aim and let go of the bomb. It crashed against the head of the trader, bounced off and hit the floor with a loud bang. The Springer was knocked unconscious. Tako counted till 10 but it remained quiet in the depot. The guard sprawled out on the floor was apparently the only one present in the storage room.

The teleporter kept Marshall's order in mind: 'The bomb must blow up in three minutes!' The incident had already cost him a precious minute.

He had a choice of an enormous variety of atom bombs of all calibers but none of them had a fuse.

He leaped down in the aisle next to the unconscious Springer. The two impulse beamers quickly changed owners and were a most welcome acquisition. With one of the bombs pressed under his arm he ran along the aisle. It was only a few steps to the next crossing between the stacks of bombs. He quickly looked left and right and found a fuse within reach of his hand.

A minute and a half had elapsed by the time he had attached the fuse to the mini-bomb. In less than a second Kakuta bounded back into the huge meeting hall where the Great Conclave of the patriarchs was assembled.

'Blast the bomb in three minutes!' John Marshall had told the teleporter, thereby setting a deadline which was fraught with danger for himself and his friends.

If they used the broad center aisle it would require at least one minute to reach the main exit provided none of the patriarchs made an attempt to hold them back. And then they had to reckon with running into the robots outside.

'We'll leave through the exit behind the platform,' Marshall whispered his order.

Once again Kitai Ishibashi gathered all his strength to blanket the crowd of patriarchs surrounding the dais with his suggestions. They were short but intensive instructions to regard their exit without undue concern.

Although a day on Goszul's Planet was longer than on Earth, Marshall used the Terranian time as his standard. It would take them 40 seconds to get to the small side exit.

The patriarchs around them were engulfed in an undiminished panic nourished by the haunting thought spreading through hundreds of brains that it was sheer lunacy to tangle with Perry Rhodan.

Tama Yokida saw a vehicle outside the long building front and utilized his telekinetic powers. The vehicle raced to him, winding around all obstacles as if driven by a top-notch expert. When it came within a couple of hundred feet, they noticed that it was occupied.

For a few seconds Kitai Ishibashi intervened again with his Strata Method. The time sufficed to make the trader in the vehicle forget his astonishment and not try to stop the vehicle. He took it in stride when the car halted in front of three strange men. He simply climbed out, greeted them and said: 'Please!'

John Marshall had counted to the end of the second minute. There were only 60 seconds left to put enough distance between them and the building when Takuta detonated the bomb.

They jumped into the car and zoomed off while Marshall listened with his inner ear to the patriarchs they were rapidly leaving behind. With his great penetrating power he perceived a mixture of fear and anger. It took him a few seconds to sort out his impressions and then he realized what events were in progress in the auditorium.

Etztak had dispatched a party from his clan to apprehend a few more victims from Levtan's men for the brainalyzer and the victims put up a stiff fight in their defense.

At this moment Kitai Ishibashi shouted for the third time: 'How much time do we have left?'

Achingly Marshall returned to the realities of his present environment. The vehicle sped past a detachment of robots. The metallic creations paid no attention to them and were merely intent on securing the main entrance.

Tama Yokida steered the hovercar and turned into a broad boulevard leading to the big spaceport when suddenly the vehicle was wrenched by a terrific invisible force and hurled up into the air.

Kitai Ishibashi's scream was drowned out by a thunderous roar.

With the death dealing bomb under his arm Tako Kakuta materialized again in the cellar under the huge assembly hall. He carefully deposited the bomb, performed another teleportation and wound up hanging high in the rafters of the ceiling, where he surveyed all participants below in one quick glance as a last situation check.

Down he went again to the cellar. The darkness didn't

bother him. There was a weak lamp shining at one end of the basement. He picked up the bomb and dashed to the light. There he was able to reecognize the time scale on the fuse.

The three minutes were up. Of this he was certain as he had an unerring sense of time.

Ignition in 10 seconds!

Thoughts of John Marshall, Tama Yokida and Kitai Ishibashi flashed through his mind. He was ready to concede that his friends were wizards who could pull off the most unlikely jobs.

The timer of the fuse was ticking away. Tako Kakuta concentrated his thoughts on his next goal and teleported himself to the spaceport.

Thora, the Arkonide woman, had quietly entered the command center of the *Stardust II*. The beautiful willowy woman was one of the few beings in Arkon's stellar empire who didn't suffer from the lethargy which caused the might of Arkon to crumble away slowly.

She looked searchingly at Khrest. The scientist silently shook his head.

'Stranded? Lost?' Her question was more of a statement, an assertion which precluded all contradiction.

Reginald Bell whirled around in his chair. 'You're mistaken!' he retorted belligerently. He was utterly disinclined to stomach the debilitating pessimism of the Arkonides, not today anyway.

'Show me proof that I'm wrong, Reginald Bell!' she

replied sharply, disregarding Khrest's pressure on her arm with which he implored her not to lose her temper.

But Thora was in no mood to control herself. She wanted to go home to Arkon and force Perry Rhodan to keep his promised word. In her excitement she failed to notice the suspicious glint in Bell's eyes. Perry Rhodan had observed it and had a good idea what kind of a harangue the irritated Bell was ready to pour out.

'Gladly, Thora,' Bell began with deceiving politeness. 'I'll prove it to you with your own claims, according to which we're uncivilized barbarians. But primitive people are much more stable and resistant than a highly bred race that has reached a state of passive existence – But, Thora, you were so eager to hear my rebuttal . . .' Bell kept grinning long after the hatch had closed again after the Arkonide woman who had fled the command center in disgust.

Apprehensively Khrest turned to Bell. 'You'll have only yourself to blame if Thora one of these days commits another of those rash acts you call a dangerous stupidity.'

Bell made a disparaging gesture and began to loll about in his chair, when the rangefinder section sounded an alarm.

The Springers had launched spaceships on Goszul's Planet. Not just a few but more than a hundred had been monitored by the rangefinder section. Everybody in the command center remembered the small atomic explosion which had taken place less than half an hour ago on Goszul's Planet.

'Structure disturbance!' the officer at the structure

sensor shouted excitedly. 'Lord, it's close!' Close meant near Goszul's Planet.

Disregarding all reason the Springer ships went into transition without consideration for the safety of the planet's inhabitants.

'Transitions are continuing without a pause!' the officer reported in growing excitement.

Now the authoritative voice of Rhodan, bringing calm to his staff was heard: 'Transition in 10 seconds! Retreat to a distance of eight light-days!'

Stardust II and Rhodan's three heavy cruisers were programmed by the positronicomputer on board the super battleship to perform transitions without the slightest delay.

... 43 ... 44 ... now three together ... 48 ...' The officer monitoring the structure sensor kept counting the transitions.

There were five seconds left for Rhodan's fleet before the execution of the short transition. The maneuver was so synchronized for the four ships as to cause only one single disturbance of space. Thus it was next to impossible for the Springers on Goszul's Planet to keep tab on the Terranian fleet's movement since the spacetime continuum was being severely strained by their own transitions.

Perry Rhodan and Reginald Bell looked at each other. The countdown had reached zero. The universe with its splendor of brilliant suns suddenly vanished for the four ships simultaneously and burst open to swallow the battleship and the three heavy cruisers in a transition.

Tako Kakuta materialized again in the command center of the *LEV XIV*.

Three traders jumped up terrified as a man suddenly appeared out of nowhere. But the terror felt was not so strong as to prevent them from reaching automatically for their weapons.

Spontaneously Tako pulled the triggers of the two impulse beamers he had seized a few minutes earlier. He shot three times. Then the ventilation system sucked three gas clouds out with a whining noise.

The teleporter spun around and now able to take his first look around. The hatch door behind him was closed. If there were other sentries posted on board the ship, they had apparently noticed nothing at all of the brief scuffle.

Tako made a quick check. Suddenly his eyes widened and he started to swear. A critical piece of equipment was destroyed – the guidance system.

In a mad rush he scanned the panoramic screen trying to find a cylindrical spaceship of the same type as the *LEV XIV*. He discovered such a ship at the other end of the spaceport.

Within a second he transported himself into the command center of the alien ship. He materialized behind a dozing Springer and knocked him unconscious with the butt of his impulse beamer before the dazed man knew what happened.

'Praised be the Arkonide technology!' Tako murmured as he pulled out the guidance system instrument with one grip of his hand. Arkonides used no wired, potentially dangerous connections, nor easily melting solder or printed circuits. The Arkonides had found simpler methods. Tako Kakuta was still enthused about their expediency when the ship was rattled by a horrendous pressure wave which buckled half a dozen support braces.

The next instant he was back on the *LEV XIV* but he was now prepared for the pressure wave. He tore the demolished set out of the console and threw it away. Then he pressed in the 'borrowed' replacement and remained unperturbed as the pressure wave reached and shook the *LEV XIV*.

'Praised be the Arkonide technology!' he murmured once again and then listened outside. The pressure wave of his atomb bomb had thundered past the *LEV XIV* without causing any damage. On the long way from the opposite end of the spaceport it had spent most of its destructive force.

Tako set out to clear the *LEV XIV* of troublesome traders. He found none and after his search went to the big airlock. He kept a sharp lookout for his friends. Suddenly he narrowed his eyes when he saw them coming and grinned. It looked like Tama Yokida. The telekin had transformed the hovercraft into a flying race car. With his extraordinary power he propelled the vehicle at fantastic speed toward the *LEV XIV*. From a height of 1000 feet he bore down on the ship of the pariahs. Tako held his breath when the vehicle failed to brake its breakneck speed close to the ground near the ramp.

The violent impact of the crash he feared never occurred. The hovercraft set down gently as a bird and Tako's comrades scrambled up the ramp in a hurry.

'Let's get out of here!' Marshall shouted. 'They're after us! Etztak is boiling mad!'

Walls crumbled like cardboard around Etztak and the ceiling came crashing down burying members of his clan under the debris.

Yet he saw and heard but little of the grisly cataclysm *Radiation!* pounded his brain; *lethal dose of radiation!*

He threw himself against a door hanging askew on its hinges and broke into a side room where a supply of spacesuits was kept. Such a suit saved him now. He escaped through the hole in the ceiling and, bucking the storm unleashed in the atmosphere, pushed through to the assembly hall. He shuddered when he saw the grim devastation wrought by the explosion as far as the eye could reach. He floated down through the hole in the ceiling, which was almost totally destroyed, and found life among the ruins. His dosimeter indicated that the radiation in this vicinity was below the danger level. He opened his helmet and grabbed the first patriarch who staggered across corpses to get outside. After he had stopped 10 or 20 people he finally found a man who had observed three men of Levtan's crew leaving the Great Conclave through the exit behind the dais.

Etztak mumbled a curse and used his spacesuit to carry himself across the hall to the platform. Among the heaps of bodies he found Levtan's documents from Perry Rhodan lying undamaged at his feet. He stuffed them hastily in his pockets and considered the find a good omen. Having a far more urgent task to pursue than remaining at the scene of the disaster he ascended in his spacesuit to the hole in the ceiling and hurried to the spaceport.

'Three of that treacherous clan have escaped!' He gritted his teeth, seething in a terrible rage. 'They've taken bitter revenge but they forgot to reckon with me! I swear I'll avenge myself as soon as I overtake them! My ship is faster...'

Etztak's hate grew by leaps and bounds and he had no inkling that John Marshall received his thought waves as if they were broadcast by a powerful transmitter.

The engines of the *LEV XIV* whined with a high pitch, piercing the ship as if lifted off the ground and soared into the clear day.

John Marshall was at the controls. Not a word was spoken in the command center. Marshall's mind was still on Goszul's Planet while his body was on board the *LEV XIV* zooming into space. He lived vicariously through the panic of the patriarchs who had survived the horrible blast of Tako Kakuta's atom bomb.

A mortal fear gripped all elders including those who resisted Kitai Ishibashi's treatment. Even the stupendous shock of the explosion – which they didn't immediately attribute to Perry Rhodan – paled beside the terror felt of his awesome power.

Tama Yokida stared at the velocity indicator as if it were his enemy. The *LEV XIV* accelerated at a miserable rate. Goszul's Planet sank away below them but only gradually changed to a sphere. In the south at the other end of the continent a far flung city appeared on the panoramic screen but was soon covered by a deck of clouds.

'Ships approaching!' Tako Kakuta called out. 'Here they come! and if I'm not mistaken they're destroyers and a big commercial vessel.'

'That's Etztak!' Marshall observed.

'How fast are they coming?' Kitai Ishibashi asked.

'Too fast to stay alive. Marshall, we'll have to fly to the side of the planet where it's night. It's our only chance. They'll shoot us down in five minutes.' Tama Yokida's voice sounded calm and unaffected by the gloomy prospects.

'Close your space helmets!' Marshall ordered.

Four destroyers and one Springer ship had taken up the chase with furious speed and were closing in on the *LEV XIV* as it desperately veered in a sharp curve to the night side of Goszul's Planet.

Altitude under 20,000 miles! It was all the engines yielded.

Marshall took time out to send a quick, condensed message in code to Rhodan. Three sentences only: 'LEVTAN DEAD. MEETING BROKEN UP WITH A-BOMB. ISHIBASHI HAS . . .'

Nothing more was received by the *Stardust II* waiting with the three heavy cruisers in a standby position eight light-days away from the Tatalira System and secure from detection by the enemy's rangefinders.

The message to Rhodan was interrupted by a heavy disintegrator beam penetrating the protective field of the *LEV XIV* and grazing the ship itself.

The aft end dissolved in glowing vapors and the forward

section of the ship plummeted down on the nocturnal side of Goszul's Planet.

At 2000 miles altitude they 'disembarked.'

Abandoning the ship was no act of senseless desperation. Their Arkonide spacesuits were self-contained tiny spaceships with propulsion and protective screens. Two thousand miles above Goszul's Planet they floated like minute grains of dust at the edge of outer space and watched the forward section of the deserted ship burn up as it collided with the denser atmosphere.

They had not abandoned the ship in a panic. Instead they had, before vaulting into space, taken time to remove a part of the equipment which had been stowed away in ingenious hiding places when the ship was being refurbished in Terrania.

Perry Rhodan's four mutants formed a chain – a chain descending into the depth. As soon as they entered the dense atmosphere they encountered jetstreams and struggled bravely against whirlwinds roaring at more than 200 miles per hour.

John Marshall drifted away. The night seemed to have swallowed him up. Kitai Ishibashi found him again and Tama Yokida brought him back with his telekinetic skill.

With the major part of their miniature generators' energy diverted to the protective screens, the spacesuits' antigrav fields operated with little power. The mutants plummeted through the first layer of clouds. Hailstones unexpectedly peppered their shields, giving them the weird feeling that they were being shot at with machinegun bullets. The clatter and vibration was very unpleasant and had a menacing feeling to it – but was preferable to the hissing of the evaporating aft end of the *LEV XIV*, a death note which still echoed in their ears.

'Caution!' Marshall warned his companions. 'We're now only 30 feet above ground.'

The falling astronauts increased the magnitude of their suits' antigrav fields and gently floated down to final stop.

They had landed again on Goszul's Planet, albeit as shipwrecked spacemen.

When the next morning dawned they activated the deflector device in their suits, causing themselves to become invisible. Although this was an inconvenience – not being able to see each other – it was preferable to being exposed to unknown prowlers. They stayed grouped together by referring to geographical reference points on the landscape.

At about 60 miles an hour they skimmed over the continent at whose southern end they had seen a spacious city during their flight the day before in the *LEV XIV*. This city was their goal as they drifted at a low altitude over the land in a southerly direction. The longer they traveled the more convinced they became that the authority of the Springers was felt to a far lesser degree in the country.

Around noon John Marshall called out excitedly: 'The city! Let's go higher where we can see it better!'

From an altitude of 1000 feet the group beheld their destination. It was an amazing sight.

'Sailing ships!' Kitai Ishibashi whispered into his

helmet and his radioed words were simultaneously heard by all his companions in their own helmets. 'Sailing ships out of the 18th century! Good Heavens, what sort of a world is this? Are these people supposed to be descendants of the Arkonides?'

Marshall interrupted abruptly, a note of great urgency in his voice: 'Quiet, please! A message from Rhodan!' His portable hypercom set was tuned in on reception. Hovering 1000 feet above Goszul's Planet, in view of a city of almost medieval appearance, Marshall intercepted their commander's short coded message:

'WAIT FOR HELP! WAIT FOR HELP!'

The call was repeated 20 times. Then communication stopped and silence was maintained throughout the rest of the day.

But it was enough. The reassuring message was all Perry Rhodan's task force needed.

To a man they knew they could rely on their leader. The Peacelord would never let them down.